THE
RESOLVE

THE
RESOLVE

C.J. SAVOIE

PALMETTO
PUBLISHING
Charleston, SC
www.PalmettoPublishing.com

Copyright © 2024 by C.J. Savoie

This book is a work of fiction. Names, characters, places and incidents are the product of the author's imagination or are used fictitiously. Any resemblance to actual events, locales, or persons, living or dead is coincidental.

All rights reserved
No portion of this book may be reproduced, stored in a retrieval system, or transmitted in any form by any means–electronic, mechanical, photocopy, recording, or other–except for brief quotations in printed reviews, without prior permission of the author.

Paperback ISBN: 979-8-8229-4261-5
eBook ISBN: 979-8-8229-4262-2

TABLE OF CONTENTS

Chapter 1: The Bank Robbery 1
Chapter 2: Rod Meets Katrina 8
Chapter 3: The Bartender 16
Chapter 4: The Bad Guys 24
Chapter 5: The Gut Feeling 31
Chapter 6: Meet Nicholas 39
Chapter 7: The Escape 48
Chapter 8: The Arrival 56
Chapter 9: The Pickup 65
Chapter 10: The Decoy 74
Chapter 11: Romance Begins 81
Chapter 12: The Assault 89
Chapter 13: The Montenegro 99
Chapter 14: Port of Mobile 108
Chapter 15: Caneco Sugar 117
Chapter 16: The Betrayal 126
Chapter 17: The Explosion 135
Chapter 18: A Deadly Shot 142
Chapter 19: Revenge 147
Chapter 20: The Costello Cartel 155
Chapter 21: A Run for It 164

Chapter 22: Cabin in the Park. 173
Chapter 23: A New Lead 182
Chapter 24: The Find 190
Chapter 25: Trust for Product 199
Chapter 26: The Parachute 208
Chapter 27: Beth Makes It 216
Chapter 28: Where's My Father? 222
Chapter 29: Miguel's Plan. 229
Chapter 30: The Vacation 236
About the Author:. 242

CHAPTER 1
THE BANK ROBBERY

The sun was up, with a few clouds in the sky, and the city traffic in downtown Jackson, Mississippi, was moderate. A slow bustle of people going to and from offices and shops along North Lamar Street filled the air with the chirps of gossip and business offers. The Union Bank and Trust, with its storefront glass panels and stately entrance columns cascading to the recessed front double doors with the brass vertical grab bars, had just opened for business at 9:00 a.m. Nicholas Musso and his long-term boyhood friend and partner in crime, Joey Palermo, sat patiently in a dark green 2001 Chevy Impala, which had a cracked rear light lens and signs of rust seeping through the faded paint on the hood, across the street from the bank. The overweight uniformed security guard sat in the foyer near the entrance doors as one of the bank tellers handed him a cup of coffee in a paper cup she had secured from the coffee shop next door. He thanked her with a half smile and offered to reimburse her, but she refused. Two well-dressed men in suits entered behind her and excused themselves as they made their way into the desk area of the loan officers and clerical section of the bank.

Joey muttered to Nicholas, "What do you think, Nicky?"

Nicholas, with his large frame and a deep, gravelly voice, turned slowly to Joey and responded in a low tone, "Give it a minute."

Joey responded, "Yeah, but I am getting nervous just sitting here."

Nicholas factually stated, "We need to wait until they all, like, settle down from their morning duties, Joey!"

A Jackson deputy patrol unit making its morning rounds passed along the street in front of the bank and turned east on East Capital Street and turned on the lights and sirens as it sped up the street to answer a radio call. Joey raised his left hand to his brow and remarked, "Boy, that was a close one!"

Nicholas returned with "Joey, they were not interested in us."

Nicholas then turned to Joey and again in a soft tone stated, "Now!"

They both descended from the Chevy and walked to the rear, where Nicholas opened the trunk as he glanced in both directions to see who was watching. Joey leaned over and ducked below the trunk cover as he reached in and grabbed a twelve-gauge automatic shotgun and a box of shells. Joey then handed them over to Nicholas and then pulled the second automatic from the trunk. Nicholas dropped a handful of shells in his side coat pocket and pulled a ski mask over his face. Joey likewise pulled his mask with his right hand while he supported the shotgun under his left arm. They both looked up and down the street as they began to run toward the bank entrance, holding the guns pointing upward. Nicholas pulled open the right door unit, and Joey dashed in, now pointing the shotgun with his finger on the trigger as he descended on the bank guard and shoved the barrel under his chin and blurted out, "Don't even think of goin' for that pistol!"

THE BANK ROBBERY

Nicholas followed behind Joey and quickly darted into the central area of the bank, raised the shotgun, fired in the air, and yelled, "This is a holdup. Everyone get on the floor!"

Women began screaming, and the men began waving their hands to quiet their screeching sounds while they helped the older ones to the cold marble floors. Nicholas fired a second shot in the air and vocalized in a heavy, boisterous voice, "On the floor, dammit!" Everyone quieted down and fell to the floor.

Nicholas approached the nearest bank teller and demanded, "Put all the cash in a bag!" The teller nervously opened the cash drawer and began stuffing a bag with bills. Nicholas fired the shotgun in the air a third time as trickling flakes of ceiling plaster floated to the floor. He shouted for everyone to put their heads down and not look up. Joey scrambled toward the front doors, clasping in his arms three bags full of loot. The escape was made without resistance out through the double doors and across the street,. They jumped into the dated Chevy Impala and drove away down the street. They pulled their masks away from their heads and headed up East Capital Street and then toward East Pascagoula Street to I-55. Sirens in the distance could be heard blaring with an approaching nearness. Nicholas half smiled at Joey with a partial feeling of gratification at their success, but it was followed with a grim look of concern as the shrill of the sirens became now more apparent.

Nicholas made a strategic move and drove past I-55, thinking that would be the most immediate focal point of the authorities' search. Nicholas and Joey's escape plan included time to make it to I-55 and head south to McComb, Mississippi, and hole up in a Motel 6 under false names for two days until the excitement of the investigation calmed down. They would then travel to Baton

Rouge, Louisiana, for a period of relaxation and time to stash their loot. However, the Jackson police were blanketing the area with patrol units. They pulled into a Circle K and topped off the Chevy with fuel while they contemplated a route south. Joey filled the tank, and Nicholas looked in the bag to do a quick count of the stashed bills. Joey had paid cash to the cashier prior to pumping, and as the pump chimed when it reached the dollar amount, he returned the nozzle to the holder and jumped back into the car. He had the obvious guilt spelled out on his face and quickly questioned Nicholas, "What is the plan?"

Nicholas, with a worried expression, looked out toward the front of the car and responded, "We need to work our way to Highway 49 and head south." Nicholas turned the key and started up the engine and pulled out.

They made it to US Highway 49 without any interference from either the local or the state police. US Highway 49 would end in Gulfport, where they could pick up I-10 and head west. They both remained quiet over the next hour and a half as they would pass an occasional state patrol unit. No one had identified their vehicle back in Jackson, and the police department was interviewing the bank personnel and outside bystanders, trying to get any description of either the robbers or the vehicle. The ski masks had completely hidden their faces, and the descriptions of the men who had robbed the bank ranged from medium-build black men to huge, burly white men with loud voices that cussed a lot. No one around had seemed to notice the vehicle in which they made their escape or what direction they were headed from the bank.

The two culprits finally arrived in Gulfport and headed west on I-10 toward New Orleans. They were feeling a little more at

THE BANK ROBBERY

ease, as no authorities appeared interested in their vehicle. They maintained the speed limits or within five miles per hour of the limits in an effort not to attract the attention of the cruising troopers. All was going well, and Joey finished counting the money and then blurted out, "It's $8,218!"

Nicholas smiled and embellished the satisfaction of their success, saying, "Not bad for a day's work."

Joey then came back with "Yeah, that will cover us for a couple of months in a life of leisure."

Nicholas then commented, "Well, I don't know about a life of leisure, but we can at least live and eat while we plan our next job." Joey leaned slightly to the left of his seat and, with the proverbial Cheshire-cat grin, responded, "What you got in mind, boss?"

Nicholas, now with a more serious expression, countered with "We will just have to plan and play it out." He continued, "Baton Rouge and those surrounding towns, like Gonzales and Plaquemine, have a lot of banks. We will just have to scope 'em out."

Joey then responded, "OK, boss; we got plenty of time."

Approximately forty-five minutes had passed, and the black of night brought on a feeling of calm until a state trooper's blue lights approached them from the rear. Nicholas, now with that sunken feeling engulfing his whole aura, blurted out, "Oh God, they got us!"

Joey, trying to resolve with another possibility, interjected, "Wait, boss—it might only be somethin' wrong with the car, or maybe you was speeding?"

Nicholas then veered the vehicle to the paved shoulder of the interstate and looked directly at Joey and with a profound tone reiterated, "No, Joey, I was not speeding!" The trooper turned on the high-intensity light mounted on his left door and announced via his patrol unit's speaker bullhorn, "Get out of the vehicle, both of you, and place your hands on the rooftop!"

Joey, with the stock of the shotgun between his legs and the barrel pointed at the floorboard, turned to Nicholas and under his breath squealed out, "I can't go back to jail, Nick!" Joey had just gotten out of the Central Mississippi Correctional Facility in Rankin County four months prior after spending three years for two counts of armed robbery of a supermarket and a convenience store in Brookhaven attached to four counts of molestation of a minor. His probation officer had been trying to locate him for the past forty-five days and had reported him missing to the state police. An added robbery of a bank would put him back in for a minimum of ten years. He was stressing over that thought when he came to the realization that the trooper would not have requested them to both exit the vehicle over a traffic violation.

Nicholas exited the vehicle thinking of his past. Although he had had no lengthy incarceration, he had spent a few nights in several local county jails for disturbing the peace, drunken disorder, and a bar fight over a woman, which had placed a smartass lawyer in the hospital with a broken jaw. As Nicholas placed his hands on the top of the Chevy, he noticed that Joey was still in deep contemplation about his next move and hadn't even opened the vehicle door. The trooper again yelled out through the speaker, "Both occupants need to exit the vehicle and place your hands on the roof!"

Nicholas screamed at Joey, "Get out, Joey—quit foolin' around." Fifteen seconds went by, and it seemed like an hour. Joey remained silent with a slight bend toward the dash and a distant stare at the shotgun still embedded between his legs.

THE BANK ROBBERY

Nicholas, realizing now that Joey had other thoughts and was frozen in his decision-making, turned toward the trooper and, in a defensive tone, with a shrill in his voice, explained, "Officer, he is scared and afraid to move!"

The trooper descended from the patrol unit, pulling his weapon, and as he crouched behind the door with the window down, he aimed the weapon and pointed at Joey through the rear window of the Chevy Impala. He again demanded that Joey exit the vehicle. Joey then turned around and looked at the officer through the rear window. He then opened the door and proceeded to exit the vehicle, leaving the shotgun on the seat with the barrel now pointed toward Nicholas. The officer was now standing on the opposite side of the Chevy, and as he approached Joey, Joey reached back in for the shotgun and in one motion fired the shotgun before the trooper was cognizant of Joey's action. Nicholas pulled away from the left side of the vehicle and commenced to the rear as he blared out to Joey, "No, Joey!" In a moment the officer looked up, bleeding from his right shoulder as he attempted to raise his weapon, and Joey fired again. Nicholas slid on his knees to the trooper's side, trying in a tense effort to stop the profound bleeding, and in a look of wonderment at Joey said to Joey, "Why, Joey?"

A second unit was pulling up to the scene, as the trooper had requested backup. He had identified the vehicle from one eyewitness at the crime scene, who was a newspaper vendor a half block up from the bank. The second trooper fired one shot in the air and demanded that Joey drop the shotgun. Nicholas, kneeling by the slain officer, chimed in with the second trooper, "Please, Joey!" Joey dropped the shotgun, and the second trooper rushed toward Joey and cuffed him as a third unit with lights flashing stopped at the rear of the first patrol unit.

CHAPTER 2
ROD MEETS KATRINA

The sky was a clear blue, and the sun was beating down on this beautiful bright day at 1 Justice Park Drive at the FBI headquarters in downtown Houston, Texas. The well-lit offices were gleaming light from the highly polished ceramic floors as the busy scuffle of the staff personnel and suited agents on phones and having group discussions could be heard. In one of the side, secluded offices with a picture glass window facing the main interior office and half viewed through the window blinds sat Chief Agent Brad Kingsworth. He was having a conversation with Rod Tillman, an energetic young agent with brown, staring, beadlike eyes that caught the female staff's attention immediately. Rod always had a serious demeanor about his casework. Brad questioned Rod and asked him if he had any leads on the source of a drug cartel funneling drugs through Laredo, Texas, from Nuevo Laredo, Mexico. It was reported that the shipments of cocaine were being transported across state lines and ending up in a remote hunting camp near Natchez, Mississippi, just outside Woodville. Rod replied, "Brad, I just got put on this case, and I am still trying to get my feet wet." Brad retorted, "Let's get a-movin,' boy. Time's a-wastin'."

Rod then got up and headed for the door and directed his attention straight at a very sexy brunette staff secretary sitting ten feet from Brad's entrance. Her name was Donna, and she had obviously always had an eye for Rod, who was tall and thin and had combed-back black hair that was just a tad too long on the neck. In fact, all the women in the clerical personnel had somewhat of an eye for Rod except Lena Fairfield, who was more interested in the other women and dressed the part, which included that hard look that gathered a few facial features in her complexion, which showed a few miles. Rod exited the door, replying to Brad in a low, mumbling tone, "First thing, boss—I'm a-movin'."

His stare was straight at Donna, who now exposed her perfectly shaped legs crossed toward Rod and said in a very sensual tone, "Good morning."

Rod then replied with his inquisitive-type voice and look, "Good morning to you, Donna." Donna was primarily assigned to Brad, or as she would acknowledge him, "Mr. Kingsworth." He was sixty-two and she was twenty-nine, and she performed most of the clerical and documentation duties for Brad but maintained a sense of independence in assisting various agents on the floor in their cases. Her goal was to become an in-house agent and provide research for other agents to help solve the intricate details from the more difficult cases. She was not interested in becoming a field agent.

Rod continued admiring her sexy knees and legs, which were enhanced by the purple open-toe spike heels she wore. He stopped at her desk and fiddled with a piece of paper. He then said in a soft voice, in referring to Brad, "He is in a mood today."

She softly questioned, "Where are you headed today, Mr. Tillman?"

He then looked up from her knees and the desk and directly into her sparkling green eyes and saw her lips gently draped across her beautiful smile and perfect teeth and responded, "Oh, the usual, to go catch a few bad guys that are on Brad's list." Rod then headed out the door and got into his assigned black Mercury four-door Marquis with black wall tires and drove off the premises in a westerly direction to pick up I-10 to San Antonio, then I-35 south to Laredo. He had a lead with a bail bondsman down in Laredo named Keenan Brucosky, nicknamed "the Brut," who had provided a $10,000 bond for a Mexican immigrant who dabbled in drugs and sold cars for his legitimate source of income. The Mexican's name was Carlos Pinetta, and he was originally from Guadalajara, near Mexico City. Carlos was indirectly involved in the transport of drugs across the Mexican border from Guatemala.

The suspected route via satellite imagery was along the coast through El Salvador to Guatemala and then to the Mexican border. Which cartel down in Colombia was the source had not been confirmed. Carlos, although not the actual carrier, did arrange all the transportation and was well compensated and always skimmed a small portion for his street operations. He had gotten caught in Laredo and was set for trial. He had bailed out to stash his cash in a more secluded location to avoid any discovery. When Rod reached Laredo, it was late evening, and he checked into a Residence Inn that he knew served breakfast at the wee hours in the morning so he could be out and about early. However, Rod was going to miss the "early birds'" breakfast because he decided to take in a bit of nightlife about Laredo's more guy-type taverns and possibly accomplish two kills at the same time. He might get a feel for the drug circulators in town and maybe meet a female companion for a change in scenery and quiet conversation.

Rod was previously married, but it didn't work out with his lifestyle in the FBI, and so it ended after three years. Fortunately, no children were involved, but his previous bride, Jennifer, was involved with a local attorney who had convinced her she needed a divorce. The divorce was complete, and after about a month, Jennifer realized that there was a much larger field of unmarried male companions on the market. She decided that the divorce attorney, whom she then learned was not getting a divorce, as he first implied, was not for her.

Rod then drove to a hot spot on the outside edge of the city called Jake's Town and Country. A modest crowd circulated around the wooden tables and chairs that enclosed a small stage where a country band was bellowing out some of the latest hits. An olive-skinned brunette with striking features stood at the mike at center stage and filled the room with her mellow country voice. Her high-heeled boots and short skirt emphasized her beautiful legs and silhouette figure, which caught Rod's eye as he entered the establishment. Rod immediately went to the bar and sat next to a woman of obvious Spanish descent who had a beautiful, welcoming smile directed at him. He pulled out the bar stool and greeted her with a nonchalant "Hello."

She responded, with a pleased look on her face, "Hello to you."

Rod, being polite, then questioned, "Are you here with someone?" and she immediately in a rhetorical fashion stated, "Yes, and he just came in." Rod's ego shot up ten points, and he then retorted back "Well, what is my date drinking tonight?"

She then, with a now-interested look in her eye, said, "I would love a margarita."

Rod looked toward the bartender and ordered a margarita and a Bud Light. He then asked her name, and she softly said, "Katrina."

"I am Rod, Katrina," he responded, and then questioned, "Are you from Laredo?"

She then stated, "Yes, I am from Laredo. I was born in Colombia, South America, but have lived in Laredo, Texas, for the last twelve years." She then asked "Where are you from?"

Rod profoundly answered, "I am a Texan, ma'am, but presently working in Louisiana."

She then inquired, "What do you do?"

He responded with a sheepish, sentimental look on his face like someone embarrassed when he said, "I am in the automobile business."

Katrina, in a quick response, said, "Oh, really?" She now had an air of a more confident demeanor and thought, well, this wouldn't be some super intelligent guy that she would have to try and keep up with versus a car salesman out on the town.

Rod then utilized the magic moment of now being relaxed to pose the question "Hey, you have any contacts for a bit of a more relaxing substance than this beer?"

She now changed mood and became suspicious and answered, "Are you undercover, trying to set me up?"

"My goodness," Rod interjected with a look of "oops" all over his face. "Seriously, do I look like an officer of the law?"

Katrina, in a coy manner, retorted, "They never do."

Rod, with a matter-of-fact look on his face, then stated, "Ma'am, if I were an undercover cop, I would not ask if there was a more relaxing venue for us to reconvene at in a leisurely fashion, now would I?"

A full emotional feeling of satisfaction now gleamed from Katrina's face, as she had fallen for Rod's total manly expressions of confidence. Rod, now trying to mitigate the scenario, then stated, "We just have to decide on a location." Rod, with a questioning look of amazement at his own immediate success, searched in his mind for the motels in the area, as he did not want to return with her to the Residence Inn, his security shelter. He then, with a voice of coolness, and gesturing with his waving arm, said, "I guess we are off to see the Wizard, Dorothy."

Katrina then reached for her purse and pulled out her cell phone and interjected with a need to Rod: "I live with my mother, and I need to call her and let her know that I may be late or maybe not home until morning—depends on whether we find this wizard of yours." She smiled and turned away, so Rod did not hear the conversation. Rod was not assuming any reason for secrecy, as he had just met Katrina and understood her possible discretionary move in quietly explaining to her mother. She then turned around and, with a full expression of acceptance of Rod with a sexual lure, said, "I am ready. Let's go." Rod, looking down at the bar tab, left a ten-spot on the bar, which included a three-dollar tip with the almost seven-dollar charge.

Rod and Katrina exited the entrance door, and Rod asked, "You want to come with me or follow?"

Katrina said "If you don't mind, I will follow if you walk me to my car over there" as she pointed to the left side of the parking lot. They walked to her 2009 white Toyota, and as he went to open her door, she reached up for his neck and kissed him in a very passionate manner. Then he felt an extreme pain in his neck as a medium-build, grizzly-type individual cracked a baton across his back, and Rod, now unconscious, fell to the ground.

Rod awakened blurry eyed from the beating about the neck. He found himself bound to a metal table in a dark, dampened room.

He glanced around and saw no one in his immediate vicinity. He began to wiggle as he tried to loosen the ties on his hands and feet. A voice from across the room in the direction of his feet blurted out, "It's no use, my friend. We've got you, Mr. FBI Man!" The voice was obviously of Spanish descent and had a slight touch in the tone suggesting that this person had had a drink or two. Rod, now on immediate defense, not understanding the reason for his kidnapping, expressed, with some anxiety in his voice, "You realize the problems you just took on by kidnapping an FBI agent?"

The uncaring concern in the voice was obvious when the abductor responded, "Señor, do you think my boss gives a damn who you work for when you come to shut his business down?" Rod, trying to get a handle on what the ultimate concern was here and now, began to correlate in his mind the issues and the connection with Katrina. She obviously didn't call her mother, and the local drug kingpin was attempting to nip the interference of the FBI with his drug sales in the bud before it destroyed his lucrative operation. The thought process now shifted to how far these nutcases were prepared to go in their point-making efforts to protect their drug business.

In the next moment, while struggling to loosen the binds on his wrists and ankles, Rod was startled by a swinging open of a metal door just behind his head as a tall figure entered the room. In his hand were a bucket of water, an electrical extension cord, and some bare copper wire. The tall man was bald headed and had tattoos up and down both arms. He had beady eyes and looked straight forward as he proceeded to remove Rod's boots and socks. Rod screamed in a voice of tense emotions, "What the hell are you doing?" The bald-headed man continued and wrapped the bare copper wire around the big toe on each of Rod's feet as he attempted, in a kicking motion and with extreme straining, to break loose of the restriction. In the following moment, he poured the water all over Rod's torso and legs. He then stuck each of the ends of the attached copper wires into receptacle end of the extension cord.

Upon that instance, the Spanish-speaking associate interjected his opinion: "You see, Mr. FBI Man, it doesn't matter what you say or do—we can fry yo' balls anytime we want to."

In the next moment, the bald-headed accomplice held up the plug of the extension cord and headed over to the electric wall socket. Rod, with a wide-eyed look on his face, blurted out in a tone of restrained energy, "Oh shit, you have lost your mind!"

Then the Spanish voice again explained, "Next time, Mr. FBI Man, we will plug it in!" And with that, the two abductors exited the room.

CHAPTER 3
THE BARTENDER

Rod, strapped to the table and still unsure of a possible return, began struggling to get free of the binds. He rolled back and forth until the table began to move and eventually fell on its edge, where now he saw other possibilities to cut the plastic ties. He moved the table with a squirming motion and reached another table that was much smaller but was displaying an assortment of tools and a various sundry of other things. He managed to tilt the table, causing the display to fall to the floor. He then eyed a pair of scissors among the items. He twisted and strained and moved himself and his anchoring load into position to finally grasp the scissors with his fingers. He intricately worked the scissors into position to cut one plastic strap and finally succeeded in getting one hand free, which then provided the means to free the rest of his limbs.

He then ran out the door and noticed where he was: on a back street in the lower-income area of Laredo. He wrote down the name of the street intersection for future reference, for research to find out who owned the warehouse. He also realized this warehouse was abandoned and the owner might not be aware of its present use. Then again, the thought came to Rod's mind that this group might have already done away with the owner. He walked several blocks until he hit a main drag and caught a taxi back to the Residence Inn.

Rod, now with his wounded pride, lay down on the bed and attempted to resolve the whole sequence of events and what had signaled Katrina. He drifted off to sleep and then awakened to sunlight glaring through the slight split in the drapes. He quickly showered and changed clothes and then called Brad at the main office in Houston. Brad answered in a frustrated voice, "Where the hell have you been? You take a vacation?"

Rod, after waiting to get a word in, responded, "No, I was hit over the head and kidnapped!"

Brad, with a concerned tone, asked, "Are you OK?"

Rod came back with "Yes, I am fine. The local drug kingpin in Laredo was trying to make an impression on me during my visit to Laredo."

Then Brad, now inquisitive, asked, "How would he even know you were in Laredo?"

Rod answered, "I am trying to make contact with a local user as a possible CI to get a line on the pipeline that may lead me back to the source."

Brad, now getting the picture, said to Rod, "Maybe you ought to come back to the office, and let's get a plan, and I will allow Troy McGinnis to give you some backup." Troy McGinnis was another field agent that had been on the force for only about two years, and experience was not his strong suit at this point in time. Rod was not happy about that idea, as it would slow him down and make him vulnerable with his inexperience should a tight circumstance occur at a most inopportune time. Rod defended his plan softly, as he knew Brad's bull-headed ideas were often difficult to alter when he got in that mood. He then continued with "Brad, before we go in that direction, would you mind if I pursue this lead alone until I get a better handle on the action here?"

Brad backed off and instead issued a warning: "Well, you had better be more alert and careful, or I will be sending an army down there to pick up the pieces!"

Rod tried to cool his anxieties by explaining, "I was caught off guard, I admit, but now I have a feel for the players and will suspect everyone."

Brad questioned, "Was there a woman in the mix, Rod?"

Rod answered in a low tone, "Yes, Brad, but it was my MO to make connections!"

Brad retorted quickly, "MO my ass. Rod, you were not thinking with the right head! Wake up and be alert. This is dangerous work, and you know better!"

Rod grabbed a biscuit and coffee at the buffet in the lobby and headed out toward downtown Laredo to the municipal government offices. He parked in a nearby parking lot and then, walking, crossed two streets and then turned right into the main double glass doors of the Webb County Courthouse. He crossed the marble lobby that had an expressed Spanish décor in the archways and heavy, detailed trim work along the walls and high ceilings. He noticed a directory on the wall near the elevators. He walked up to the directory and saw "Assessor, John G. Wilkins—fourth floor, rooms D, E, F." Rod pushed the elevator button, and the door immediately opened as if the elevator were waiting for him. He traveled to the fourth floor and searched the doors for D. He approached the door and pushed it open to a large room, which was busy with six or seven clerical people carrying paper and another five or six sitting at cubicle desks,

THE BARTENDER

buried in their thoughts. Straight in front of him was a long wooden counter with a glass shield and slotted openings for the staff to address the public.

Rod walked up to the second window from the left, where a beautiful auburn-haired woman with very pronounced features stared right into his eyes. Her eyes were crystal green, and her smoothed, soft facial features lured Rod's thoughts away from his mission for the moment. He walked up and greeted her with "Good morning," and she softly answered "Good morning. Can I help you?"

He said, "Yes, I am Rod Tillman, and I am with the FBI" as he displayed his shield and ID, with a delay in his speech because he was distracted as he focused on her beautiful red lips, which were outlined perfectly across her perfect row of white teeth. "I, ah, ah, ah, need to locate a tract of property at the intersection of Cortez Street and McClelland Avenue on the southwest corner." She then motioned for him to come to the door on the left, which was an entry into a side room with a large table in which to place a map. Rod entered through the door, now in full view of her neatly pressed tan blouse, dark skirt, and heels, and he observed that her name was embossed on a shiny gold nameplate pinned to her blouse: Ellen Williams. She next explained that he could show her the location on a map that was framed on the wall and included the entire Webb County, which mostly included the City of Laredo. The coordinates illustrating sections and townships were outlined on the map, and she could then narrow it down to a defined location before going to the records to search for property ownerships. The assistant cross-matched the street intersection with section coordinates and responded to Rod, "Now I can go to the file locations and find out the past sales and ownerships." She then proceeded into the main file room, with Rod remaining in the map room, contemplating his next plan of action to follow the trail of his perpetrators. She returned with a gleam in her eye. Rod not sure if it was an affectionate flirt toward him or just her being cheerful and helping. She showed Rod a book of surveys for the property and the last owner. A Paul Champane was listed on the survey. Rod couldn't help but notice the iconic surveyor's name and seal on the bottom left-hand corner of the very formal-looking survey: "IDEAS." It was spelled out below as "Intricate Design Engineers and Surveyors." He then asked Ms. Williams if she had an address on Mr. Paul Champane, and she reviewed the documents in the folder further and then informed Rod that he paid the taxes from an address in Dallas, Texas. She then recited the address as 2213 Commerce Street, Dallas, Texas.

"Is there a phone number?" Rod questioned.

She answered, "Yes, but I do not know if it is current." She then enumerated, "The number is area code 214, 555-1212." She ended with "Will that be all, Mr. Tillman?" as she once again smiled with a glow in her beautiful green eyes.

He then responded with "Yes, ma'am. You have been extremely helpful, and I may be calling on you again."

She then answered "Anytime, Mr. Tillman," and he then blurted back, "Call me Rod!" She now became even more interested when she replied, "Yes, Sir Rod." Rod then departed from the assessor's office and took the elevator back to the first floor.

Rod then headed back to the Residence Inn to contemplate his next move of whether to head to Dallas and track down Mr. Paul Champane or have Brad send Troy McGinnis on a field trip to locate Mr. Champane. Rod called Brad back and requested he now bring Troy into play. Rod explained the details of Mr. Champane and the case, and Brad sent Troy on a search-and-find mission. Troy, thirty-three years old and of medium stature, with light sandy hair and brown eyes, was anxious to get involved and get out into the field. While Troy made his plans to head to Dallas, Rod decided to go back Jake's Town and Country and see if he could run into Ms. Katrina and her band of tricksters. It was now nearing 4:00 p.m., and the locals didn't really begin to appear on the scene until around 6:00 p.m., after work. The "heel kicking" and noise levels didn't increase until about 7:00, after a few beverages had been consumed. However, Rod wanted to use this quiet time to obtain some possible information and identities.

He drove up and entered the bar, where he noticed the barmaids straightening tables and getting ready for the influx of regulars in a short period of time. He then turned and headed toward the long bar where he vividly remembered meeting Katrina, and he observed the bartender wiping the countertop and fiddling with condiments. He addressed the tall, lanky, thirty-year-old man in a white shirt and black vest with sleeves rolled up for work. Rod then asked the bartender if he remembered him from the previous night, and after a pause, he responded with, "Yeah, I remember you were sitting about right there with that Mexican girl."

"Yes," Rod retorted, "and you wouldn't know who she was?"

He then answered, "She has been in here several times over the past few months, but I remember you left with her and y'all never came back."

Rod looked at him straight on and then questioned, "Ah, what is your name?"

The bartender hesitantly responded, "Joe, Joe Gillien." The bartender then continued, "Are you some kind of cop?"

Rod then pulled out his badge and stated, "I am with the FBI, and I am in Laredo on assignment."

The bartender then asked, "Is that woman some kind of illegal?"

Rod then immediately responded, "Well, something like that. Do you ever remember her being in here with anyone else?"

The bartender, now becoming a bit frustrated with all the questions and worried other patrons might get annoyed, responded with an emphatic tone to Rod, "I think I have answered enough of your questions, and if you are not in here to buy a drink, Mr. FBI, then I think it is time for you to go!"

Rod, not appreciating his demeanor, looked to the right softly in an effort to see who was watching or even paying attention, then returned with one swift motion and grabbed, with both hands, the bartender's vest and pulled him face to face and in a matter-of-fact voice answered, "I can shut this place down and have your ass down to headquarters and repeat all these questions, if you would like!"

The bartender, now wide-eyed with fear, renewed his thoughts and composure and then responded "Ah, ah, she, ah, has been in here a couple of times, and usually she meets different guys here. Ah, they drink and sit at that table over there" as he pointed across the room to a table in the corner. Now Rod pulled out an ID card that had his name and cell phone and was embossed in bold letters with "FBI agent" and a Houston address. He then explained in a low tone, "Now, you listen, Joe Gillien. You take this card with my cell phone number on it, and the next time this Mexican woman comes in, you give me a call, OK?" And then Rod looked at him straight in the eyes and stated, "Now, Joe, if she comes in and you happen to forget to call me, and I find out, well, that's considered obstruction of justice, and I am going to arrest you and then haul your ass in!" and ended with "Do we have an understanding, Joe?"

Joe, the bartender, shook his head in a motion of total comprehension of the agent. Rod then said, "Now I will have that beer!"

Rod realized that all the present although low-voiced conversation was a possible provocation for any onlookers to overhear and report back to the previous perpetrators. He sat for a while and scanned the room for such persons that might appear as suspicious characters. He then decided it would be best to depart the premises and return another night and be less conspicuous, especially to the bartender. Timing would also play a role in his being observed. Rod then headed out to his vehicle, looking over his shoulder before driving away.

CHAPTER 4
THE BAD GUYS

Troy McGinnis drove into Dallas proudly dressed in a gray flannel suit, white shirt, and dark blue striped tie and parked on the street across from 2213 Commerce Street. He eyed the entrance of a three-story brick building; the numbers imprinted on the glass entrance were the address of Mr. Paul Champane, Real Estate and Commercial Properties, Inc. Troy entered the building and saw the business name in bold polished-brass letters at the top of the wall, mounted directly to the right side of the elevators. The office was the whole third floor. Troy stepped into the elevator and pushed the number three, and in a moment the doors opened into a very gaudily decorated waiting area. As he stepped out, a secretary staring straight at him sat astutely at her desk. The secretary was the typical thirty-five-year-old "blond bomber," chewing gum and dressed in a pink, tight knit sweater, her hair pinned up with curls dangling over her large white hooped earrings. She greeted Troy with "Can I help you, sir?"

Troy, in a very professional tone and anxious to flash his FBI badge for the very first time, responded, "Yes, I am Troy McGinnis with the FBI, and I am here to see Mr. Paul Champane," as he brandished his picture ID with the attached bright brass shield on the other leaf of the fold-out leather pouch.

The secretary, now curious, but with a somewhat concerned look that usually brings on facial tension, questioned, "Is he expecting you, Mr. McGinnis, and can I tell him what this is in reference to?"

Troy immediately, in a trained response, replied, "It is just some routine questions about some property he owns in Laredo, Texas, and no, I do not have an appointment."

She then picked up the phone and dialed 1 and 0 on the intercom line, and Mr. Champane answered with a "Yes."

She, in an emphatic tone, said, "There's a Mr. Troy McGinnis with the FBI, and he would like to speak with you."

Mr. Champane then questioned, "What about?"

She responded, "He says it is about some property you own in Laredo."

Champane then told her, "Well, tell him to have a seat, and I will be out in a minute." She then instructed Troy to have a seat and said that Mr. Champane would be out shortly.

Troy then took a seat in the small entrance lobby on the vinyl loveseat situated between two end tables with lamps. He grabbed an outdated magazine and began flipping pages as the secretary looked down at her painted nails with a look of boredom. Mr. Champane, in the back office, was now on the phone, obviously talking to someone in reference to the warehouse in Laredo and questioning why was the FBI visiting him. Mr. Champane was a medium-height, overweight, and out-of-shape man in his early sixties. His round face was red with frustration, and this magnified his oily, long, combed-back silver hair. He was wearing dark blue slacks and a light blue plaid sports coat with an open-collar white, but somewhat wrinkled, button shirt. The minute turned into twenty-five minutes, and now Troy was becoming impatient and gave the secretary a half smile from the side of his mouth. She was now in a moment of embarrassment because of the delay and wanted to call Mr. Champane back to hurry him along but held off the urge. She interjected to Troy, "I'm sure he will be out shortly" as she noticed phone light from his previous call had now been off for over five minutes. Fifteen more minutes dragged by, and now Troy, in an agitated posture, stood and in a demanding tone demanded that she go and check and see what was keeping Mr. Champane.

She abruptly rose from her chair and replied, "Just wait here, and I will check." She darted through the office hallway door and disappeared. In less than three minutes she returned, and with her hands raised, she stated, "He is gone. He has left." Troy, now really angry, forced his way through the same door and looked in all the empty offices down the hallway corridor. He opened the door to Mr. Champane's office and saw the vacant desk. He searched the surroundings of the office and found nothing. He noticed scribbling on a sticky note near the phone with the letter K and a phone number. He bypassed the secretary, who was effortlessly trying to keep him from investigating the scene. He then went to the back of the office to a door that was an access to the rear fire escape.

He questioned the secretary, "Where does this door go?" and she responded, "To the stairway that goes out to the parking lot."

He then asked, "What kind of vehicle does Mr. Champane drive?"

She, now with a look of panic, blurted out, "A silver GMC pickup truck."

Troy then asked "Is it new? Do you know what year and model?"

She then stated, "It is a 2014 because he just had me give that information to the insurance company."

Troy then mumbled "Thanks" and raced through the door and descended down the two flights of stairs and into the parking lot. There was no sign of the 2014 GMC silver pickup truck.

The following night, Rod again arrived at Jake's Town and Country and parked his Marquis in a very unnoticeable location, but still in perfect view of the bar front door, as he had decided to sit in the parking lot and stake out the bar and the patronage going in and out of the entrance. After an hour he noticed something unusual about three men entering the bar, as they appeared to be two bodyguards in protection of an older, out-of-shape man of Spanish descent with a mustache. They went in as if they owned the place, bypassing everyone in their way. Rod exited the vehicle and returned to the bar and tried to remain unnoticed as he sat at a small table in a dark corner. The three suspects went to the exact table the bartender had pointed out and ordered cocktails. Five minutes expired, and like expected rain, in walked Katrina, decked out to the max, and she approached the suspect's table. She didn't notice Rod, as he looked downward, remaining inconspicuous. Katrina walked up to the table and bent over and kissed the patriarch being guarded, and then she sat next to him. The relationship between her and the older gentleman was definitely not a paternal one, but more of as if she was his concubine.

Rod gave them a moment to solidify the greeting, during which he took the time to survey the bar and possibly maintain his surprise entrance. He looked around the room and didn't detect any other suspicious individuals that would be a party to his suspects. Rod then slowly approached the table of the four, and as Katrina looked up with a stare of fear combined with a total loss for words, she tried to hide. Rod, with one hand on his holstered revolver and his other hand flipping out his FBI insignia and badge, demanded to all at the table, "Please, remain seated and do not draw any weapons. I am FBI agent Rod Tillman, and all of you are under arrest!" In an instant, one of the bodyguards reached for his weapon as the boss man, Mr. Lucas, put his hand on the bodyguard's hand and indicated to him to remain calm. In a like effort, the other guard had pulled his weapon halfway out when Rod extracted his weapon and put it to the aggressive guard's head and stated, "Ah, I don't think you want to do that. I have cause to arrest Katrina and not the rest of you unless you are associated with the assault and battery of an FBI agent." He continued, "I have now contacted the local police department, and they will be arriving shortly to incarcerate Ms. Katrina." The obvious other three associates remained silent, as they were almost totally in unexpected amazement. Just as Rod handcuffed Katrina, the boss man stood up and questioned Rod in an attempt to water down the whole matter. Rod, with gun in hand, shut him down immediately with a warning response: "Sir, if you don't sit down, then I can only assume you have knowledge of Ms. Katrina's involvement in a felony crime. Is that so?"

The boss man immediately went silent and sat back down as he looked at Katrina with a reflection of "What have you done?" The other two bodyguards had an anxious expression of "Let's take this one-man smartass out and get out of here," but the boss man, with arms spread to both guards, stated, "Leave it."

Within minutes, the Laredo Police Department arrived on-site, and four police officers in uniform barged into the bar. They observed the scene and pulled their weapons and approached the table.

Rod flashed his badge and turned over Katrina to them in cuffs. One officer questioned Rod, "Do you want to take these other three clowns in?"

Rod, in a sarcastic tone, responded, "Nah, it won't be long before I come for them." Rod then rolled his eyes from the three to the police officer. The officer then escorted Katrina out of the bar. Rod turned back to the boss man and his goons and threatened him with "I don't know what your connection is to Katrina, but I assure you I will investigate, and if necessary I will track you down, and if you are connected, then that will, well, let's just say make my week."

In a return comment by the boss man, he calmly, in a Mafia godfather demeanor, explained to Rod, "Maybe, officer, you don't know who you are dealing with, and you may be disappointed in what you investigate, but surely you will be sorry you threatened me."

Rod now, with an authoritative air, returned to the boss man with a response: "I truly hope you continue to threaten me with what I already suspect." Rod then turned and walked out of the bar, keeping his right hand on his weapon.

Rod pulled his vehicle up to the Residence Inn. He sat for a moment and stared into the darkness. In the moment of total silence, his passenger door window was shattered by a gunshot! The explosion of tempered glass caused Rod to jump and pull his door handle as he fell out of the driver's side of the car. He remained down in a squatted position with his weapon now poised to aim and shoot. A minute passed, and no additional shots were fired. Rod slid upward on the side of the vehicle and surveyed the surrounding area. The parking lot, half filled with vehicles, projected a sense of total calm. Rod's eyes scanned the whole lot, searching for a brake light, expecting a departure of the assailant, as the gunshot was an obvious warning to scare him off. His expectation was realized when he heard screeching tires across the lot, which was the result of a vehicle pulling out of the parking lot and heading toward the interstate. Rod tried to get an identity, but the darkness overshadowed that possibility. He was now concerned with the fact that they knew his location and probably had a stakeout nearby, expecting him to relocate. He decided to remain at the Inn and knew they were done for the night.

CHAPTER 5
THE GUT FEELING

Rod headed toward his room at the Residence Inn, walked in, and fell back on the king-size bed. He then pulled out his cell phone and punched in Troy's cell. No one answered after about six rings. He then put the phone down on his side, and in that instant it rang. The call was Troy returning his call. Troy attempted to explain why he didn't answer Rod's call but was interrupted by Rod asking, "How did you make out with Mr. Champane?"

Troy responded, "He snuck out the back before I could question him."

Rod retorted, "Oh, that's just great!" Then Rod asked, "Did you have a chance to see or find out where he might be headed?"

Troy responded again, "No, but I did find out he is driving a 2014 GMC silver pickup truck."

Rod sarcastically exclaimed, "Well, that should narrow it down to about five million in Dallas!" Rod then instructed Troy to meet him in Laredo by noon the next day. He then remarked, "We need to go and check that warehouse out again. I think that is the connection to all this smuggling with our cast of characters in this case."

Troy then sheepishly said, "I could try and track down Champane here in Dallas. I can pressure that dingy secretary and maybe find out his hangouts around here."

Rod then, in a suspicious tone, stated, "I have a feeling that Mr. Champane is heading to Laredo to check out the screwups down here. In any case, I have Katrina in custody, and my vehicle's side window has been blown out, and now they know where I am residing at present. I need to relocate."

Troy then responded, "Well, OK, I am heading your way. Where do you want me to meet you?"

Rod replied, "Call me when you get close, and I will let you know. I may be at the local hired guns', asking Katrina a few questions." Rod hung up and headed to the shower, not really worrying that the assailants would return, as he thought those were warning shots to let him know they were on to him and could get to him at any time. His suspicion of Katrina varied in his thoughts. He knew she was connected but felt it was not by choice. He kept feeling there was more to her fake loyalty, but fear played a large part and controlled her actions. His questioning of her would have to provide some means for her escape from Gus Lucas and his cartel.

Rod opened his eyes from the king-size bed and saw the sparkle of sunlight beaming from the crack of the seam of the pulled drapes. He checked his cell phone on the side table and noted the time, 7:13 a.m. He sat up, stretched, got out of bed, and headed for the bath. It was now 7:55 a.m., and as he walked out the room door, he headed to the elevator, thinking about that shattered glass window on his vehicle. He couldn't drive around it in that condition. He walked into a breakfast area and saw a room half filled with guests dining on the hotel-provided eggs, biscuits, and

THE GUT FEELING

waffles. He then decided to head toward the check-in desk and ask if there was an auto glass repair shop nearby. The result was there was, and now they were on their way to pick up his vehicle to have it repaired. He then contacted the auto rental company and requested another vehicle. Once he got past all the arrangements for new travel, he sat down in the breakfast community of tourists and had a cup of coffee and a biscuit and then called Chief Agent Brad Kingsworth.

Rod explained to Brad all the recent events and that Troy was on his way to meet him. Brad, somewhat questioning the sequence of all the past events and now Rod's agenda for this now unknown future, asked, "Rod, what is your plan? I mean, you got Troy headed over there, but you are not even sure of all the players and what they are planning. What gives?"

Rod then responded, "You know me, Brad—it has always been my gut on these cases. I think Troy can watch my back and allow me time to check these guys out!"

Brad, with a sigh, said, "All right, Rod, but you had better start giving me something I can send up the ladder."

With that Rod then left it with "You got it, Brad—just give me a little time" and pushed the off button. Rod then, in his new car rental, headed over to where Katrina was being held. He walked into the station and straight to the caged check-in desk and flashed his badge, introduced himself, and stated that he was there to interrogate Katrina. The desk clerk officer flipped through his arrest list for the day and then picked up the phone and stated to the receiver, "That FBI guy is here." He then buzzed the locked door open and told Rod to go down a hallway, after which he turned and pointed to the rear and said, "Straight down to the end of that hallway."

Rod walked into a conference room where Katrina was seated with a distant look to the side, as if to say she wasn't going to answer any questions. He sat down across the table, and the attending officer stepped out of the room. Rod looked directly at Katrina and asked, "Well, you want to tell me who those guys you were with in that bar are?" Katrina remained silent. Rod then asked Katrina, "Do you realize the trouble you are already in for? Assault on a federal agent?"

Katrina then blurted out, "Gus will get me out!"

Rod then questioned, "Gus?" and then Katrina defensively stated, "Yes, Gus, and you have no idea who you are dealing with!"

Rod then explained, "Katrina, I don't think that Gus is going to be able to help you when we ship you out of here to a federal facility up north."

Katrina then, with a really worried look, cried, "What do you mean, ship me out of here? I didn't shoot anybody!"

Rod then replied, "Yeah, but you are an accessory to assault and battery of a federal agent, and we know about the drug smuggling."

Katrina then tried to play the innocent-woman card and blurted out, "I don't know what you are talking about!"

Rod, with his cell phone buzzing, replied, "OK, Katrina, you are refusing to cooperate, so I guess we will get the paperwork started." Rod then stood up and answered his cell phone as he walked out of the room. The call was from Troy, asking where Rod wanted him to meet him, as he was driving in on I-35. Rod told him the exit and how to get to the station. He then explained that he was not getting much out of Katrina, but he thought he knew now who one of the ringleaders was. He asked, "Do you remember the Colombian relative of Pablo Escobar named Gus something that had come up on the radar for drug smuggling?"

THE GUT FEELING

Troy, with his wanting-to-be-involved demeanor, responded to Rod with "Yeah, yeah, he was starting up his own cartel somewhere in Central America."

Rod then ended with "Meet me here, and then we will drive to Champane's warehouse."

Gus Lucas, as he was nominally called in the drug underworld of the Americas, was connected to the Pablo Escobar drug family but had escaped when the forces started to cave in around the cartel. No one knew where he had disappeared to, but he now was back on the scene and was meeting with Paul Champane at the warehouse at the intersection of Cortez and McClelland Streets. Champane, in a raised tone, was stressing to Gus Lucas that the FBI was now sticking its nose right in the middle of all their affairs. Gus, with a cool and controlled mannerism, replied to Champane, "I know, Señor. The FBI is here, and they have dragged my Katrina away from me, but she won't talk." He then continued, "We must not get too excited—we always will be under suspicion."

Champane then, with a defensive tone, replied, "Yes, but they know where this warehouse is located."

Gus then replied, "Of course they do—this is where my boys warned the FBI agent that if he hung around, his life would be very vulnerable."

Champane then excitedly questioned, "Are you crazy? You brought him here to threaten him and did not kill him?"

Gus then, in a low tone and with a look of a methodical plan being devised in his mind, said, "Well, it is all in the plan, Señor Champane."

Champane then asked, "You have a plan that includes the feds and you haven't let me in on it?"

Gus then turned and looked at Champane with his beady eyes and replied, "I have a plan, but first I must get my trusted commandant and one of the most talented artists in the world of planning out of prison."

Champane now, with a look of total confusion, inquired of Gus, "And this is?"

Gus, in in a low tone, responded, "My good friend Mr. Nicholas Musso."

Champane, now with worry written on his face, then questioned Gus while shaking his head: "You are now telling me you want to help a criminal named Musso, Gusso, or whatever from prison to assist you in some plan, and I am just now hearing of this?" He continued, "What happened to the transfer of drugs through my warehouse to the distributors we first talked about?"

Gus then, with a look of calm, stated, "Señor, the movement of such goods is not that easy, and many doors are now open to the federals, which is always expected, but we must always have an alternate plan when preparing to move these costly items for sale. Do you not agree?"

Champane then turned and scanned the room guarded by the associates of Gus and sarcastically replied, "Maybe so, Gus, but if your plan includes such a strategy, why wasn't I informed from the beginning?"

Gus then turned and in a low, deep tone, with a look of indifference, explained, "Well, Mr. Champane, because you have served your purposes!" A gunshot rang out from across the room from one of the tall associates. The mark hit Mr. Champane squarely in the

THE GUT FEELING

upper temple. Champane now, with a look of total surprise, fell, grabbing the back of a chair and crumbling to the floor.

Two hours passed, and now the warehouse was clear except for Champane's dead body lying on the floor with the bullet in his head. Rod and Troy, pulling up to the warehouse, noticed a crack in the side door and the lock not in place. They descended from the rental car with weapons pulled and approached the warehouse and entered through the unlocked door. Upon their entrance, they immediately noticed the body on the floor across the room. Rod searched the room with his eyes, and Troy, in his professional demeanor, moved slowly from post to post, checking all angles and side views for a possible surprise attack. However, all was quiet, and Rod knelt to check the neck pulse of the slain man while maintaining his vigilance with his weapon still in the raised position. Troy now carefully viewed the body of the dead man on the floor and with a look of some surprise questioned, "Is that Champane?"

Rod, with an eye roll, responded, "How would I know, Troy? I've never met the man."

Troy then answered, "Well, the only reason I say that is there is a 2014 silver GMC parked up by the corner."

Rod then pulled out of the inner pocket of the man's sport coat a wallet with his identification information. "This is our man Paul Champane of Dallas, Texas."

Troy, with a bit of wonderment, interjected, "Why would they shoot him if he was the owner of the warehouse, which is, I would suppose, the storage station for housing their stash before distribution."

Rod then also questioned in disbelief, "Yeah, why would they do that?" Rod then pulled out his cell phone and called the local sheriff's office and stated they needed to send the coroner and a unit to transport Paul Champane's body to the morgue. He also referenced that this was a murder scene and they would have to conduct an investigation. Rod then addressed Troy: "We should remain here until the locals arrive."

Troy replied, "Definitely, and we don't know if any of the Lucas gang will return."

Rod, in his usual demeanor, with his typical eye roll, interjected, "No, I don't think they would want to expose any further their obvious involvement."

While they were in conversation, a local patrol unit pulled up outside the warehouse. Rod descended from the warehouse and greeted the officer, flashing his badge, as he explained the status. Rod and Troy then left the site somewhat perplexed.

CHAPTER 6
MEET NICHOLAS

Nicholas Musso, in his prison garb, an orange jumpsuit with stenciled black print across the back signifying the Texas Department of Corrections and an identification number, stared at the cell wall. The door was open, and prisoners milled about in groups of two or three, mostly with depressed, daunting expressions written across their faces. The loud screeching sound came from the loudspeaker; that was the standard warning signal that an informative message was about to be delivered to the populace. The message was notifying that Nicholas Musso, prisoner number 1509, had a visitor and was to report to the assembly station and see Officer Mackenny at the desk. Nicholas, with a look of subdued surprise, raised his left eyebrow as a question because over the last two years he had received only two visitors. One was the court-appointed attorney, and the other was his brother looking for papers to be signed releasing the family home for possible sale back in Chicago. He then stood up and headed to the stairway leading down to the prison chamber entrance and met the guard at that locked, barred door. He addressed the guard with "Ah, I am Musso. They said I had a visitor."

The guard then turned his head to his shoulder intercom and in a low tone stated, "I have Musso here for the visitor."

A response was returned through the mounted shoulder speaker: "Send him through."

The prison was located on Twelfth Street in Huntsville, Texas, and had the nickname "Walls Unit" and was the oldest criminal incarceration facility in the state, with its first inmates arriving on October 1, 1849, before the Civil War. The prison had the most active execution chamber in the administrative headquarters of the Texas prison system. All the Texas Department of Corrections' permanent records were located in these buildings. The red brick walls made this icon of prison stand out in this, the county seat of Walker County. Huntsville had a population of over forty thousand in the metro area, having first been founded in 1836 as an Indian trading post. Sitting in the visiting area of this infamous prison, waiting on Nicholas Musso, sat Victoria Lucas with her smooth olive complexion and long, dark hair.

Nicholas walked in with an air of some confusion mixed with thoughts of defense should this be another lawyer. He spanned the spectrum of the room and saw at the assigned table this very attractive woman with her beautiful tanned legs crossed for a full view. As he proceeded toward the table, he thought, Well, at least they are getting creative in who they send to defend me. His first words were "You here for me?" and she responded, "In a manner of speaking."

He then retorted, "Well, I must say you are the best-looking person to visit me in the last two years." He paused and then continued, "So what are you, a lawyer?"

She moved her right index finger in a circle near the edge of the table and after a deep breath questioned, "You know a man named Gus Lucas?"

Nicholas reluctantly answered, "Maybe, who wants to know?"

MEET NICHOLAS

She then, in a low tone, smoothly replied, "I am his daughter, Victoria Lucas, and I have a proposal for you."

Nicholas, after looking both left and right to determine if anyone else nearby might be listening, and being curious about the notion that this might be some sort of setup again, questioned, "Oh really?"

Victoria, now realizing that Nicholas was feeling somewhat vulnerable across the table and that some sign of proof should now be forthcoming, stated, "Look, you don't know me, and I understand your reluctance here, but my father sent me because he doesn't trust anyone else and he needs your help."

Nicholas, now in a curious mode, asked, "How can I help your father? I am in a state prison, or haven't you noticed?" He waved his hands in a circular fashion and rolled his eyes and then again said, "Hello?"

Victoria then continued with a cautious tone in both her voice and her demeanor. "My father wants you out of here and has a plan to get you out of here." And then she added, "I am not prepared to lay that plan out just now. My purpose for this meeting is to get an understanding and see first how you feel about this."

Now Nicholas, staring straight into Victoria's eyes with a sense of both excitement and yet disbelief, responded, "What is so important that a man like Gus Lucas would want to get me out of prison?" And then he mentioned, "Me and Gus go back to when we pushed a little weed and a little dis and a little dat across the line, but getting me out of here, it must be big." His eyes continued to scope out the surrounding area. Nicholas, with a bucketload of doubt, questioned, "Is that all you are going to give me and get my hopes up?" Then he persisted: "Why? And what part do I play in this?" Then a minute of silence prevailed as both sat and stared at each other.

Then, leaning back in her chair and crossing her sexy long legs and next folding her arms and tilting her head slightly, she questioned, "So are you in or are you out?"

Nicholas, staring straight at her beautiful legs in the spike heels, replied, "When I last checked, my schedule was pretty open for the next couple of months, so I guess I am in."

Then Victoria, getting up from the chair, moved behind and placed both hands on the back of the metal frame and with a proud sense of accomplishment shifted her chin upward and grinned and relayed, "Then we will be in touch." She then turned and headed for the exit. Nicholas continued to watch her movements all the way to the guard at the entry door. Victoria departed from the front of the Texas prison with her cell phone to her ear. She then ended the conversation with "Pick me up." In less than a minute, a black Lincoln with tinted glass windows pulled up in front, and the back door swung open, and she climbed in and pulled the door closed. She stared up at the front passenger side of the vehicle, and with her beauty glistening, she informed the passenger, "He's in."

———※———

Rod and Troy were now each looking down at their mugged beers at a table back at Jake's Town and Country Tavern, and after a moment of silence, Troy questioned, "Why kill Champane in his own warehouse?"

Rod, with an inquisitive look, then attempted to answer Troy: "Probably to throw us off and make us think that Gus Lucas gave up and left town, leaving no witnesses."

MEET NICHOLAS

Troy, in a myopic, expressive tone, then replied, "Well, we know better than that."

Rod with a sarcastic tone and in a lazy voice then said, "No, they didn't fool us!" Rod then redirected his thoughts and told Troy, "Look, we need to track down Lucas and get a tap on his whereabouts." He then continued, "Troy, visit the locals and see if they have any ongoing surveillance on our boy and whatever they might be forthcoming with." Rod then followed with "And Troy, don't overdo the FBI thing and put them in a defensive mood. Remember, a little honey and niceness goes a long way."

Troy then, with a you-can-count-on-me expression, responded, "I got this, Chief. Have a little confidence!"

Rod ended with "I think I will go have another conversation with Ms. Katrina."

Troy questioned, "Didn't she get bailed out by Mr. Lucas?"

Rod then in response stated, "Yep, but the bondsman has to have an address." Rod and Troy then retreat from the table, and Rod instructed Troy, "Catch that tab and give her a decent tip," and he finished with "I'm sure we will be coming back here real soon!"

Troy answered, "I got it!"

Gus Lucas sent one of his head henchmen with $10,000 in cash to bail out Katrina. Katrina walked out, a felon for assaulting a federal agent. She was extremely frightened as she was now transported by the henchman back to Gus Lucas's residence. When they arrived, Gus walked out and opened her door and gave her a big hug, and he confirmed to her, "Relax—you have nothing to worry about!" and then reaffirmed, "That FBI man is after me, not you!" He then instructed her, "Go inside and get something to eat, and my man will take you home."

She then responded, "Mr. Gus, I just want to go home and clean up."

Gus, with a wave of his hand, gestured to the henchman: "Take her home." She got back into the vehicle, and they drove off.

Brad, after being informed, per the protocol, of Katrina's release, called Rod and in a frustrated tone informed him, "Well, your chief witness is out on bail."

Rod in a subtle voice replied, "Well, I kind of knew it wouldn't take long." Rod then, with a sense of encouragement, stated, "You know, Brad, this may actually help us in our investigation."

Brad questioned, "And how?"

Rod then in a positive manner instructed, "Her fear in the free world may be exactly what we need!"

Katrina walked out of her small suburban house with a bag of trash and put it in a curbside garbage can. She looked around to see if anyone was watching. Rod, sitting in his vehicle up the street, remained still, with his beady eyes staring directly at Katrina. She did not notice him and placed the cover over the can and headed back toward her house. Rod waited another five minutes and then exited the vehicle and walked up to the door. He knocked, and there was no response. Rod then called out, "Katrina, it is FBI agent Tillman—please open the door." Inside, Katrina panicked and stood silent in her kitchen doorway, trying to decide whether she should ignore the knock or concede to answer. Rod continued, "I know you are in there. I just watched you dump your trash."

Katrina then realized the futility of not responding and then opened the door. She then looked at Rod with an I-don't-give-a-damn expression and questioned, "Are you following me?"

Rod in a sarcastic manner answered her, "Gee, that is a great observation, Katrina, and yes, I need to ask you a couple of more questions. I can do that from out here, or you can allow me in and we can sit and talk. I am not here to arrest you," Rod explained. He then continued, "But there has been a murder, and your help may get you a get-out-of-jail-free card—who knows?" Katrina, with a suspicious look on her face, and at the same time thinking she should not close the door, which would give the appearance of not cooperating, opened the door wider and stood aside. Rod then walked in and searched for a setting to have a conversation. He headed straight to the kitchen and sat at the table.

Katrina, in a formulated, hospitable gesture, asked, "Do you want something to drink, Mr. FBI Man?"

Rod replied, "No, just talk."

Katrina accentuated her feminine features, as if such was a matter of habit, and positioned herself in the chair opposite and across the table and then looked at Rod with those big brown eyes and draping long hair and questioned, "What do you want to know?"

Rod asked immediately, "Who murdered Mr. Champane in the same warehouse where you and your cohorts kidnapped me and tried in your little house of horrors to scare me off?"

Katrina now, with a deep look of concern, responded, "Who is Mr. Champane, and what are you talking about, murder?"

Rod was not quite sure if this is was an act to throw him off or if she was really not involved with this part of Mr. Lucas's criminal activities at this level. He then questioned further, "How did you come to know Mr. Lucas?"

Katrina now, with a sympathy-for-me reaction, began with "Well, I was alone and trying to earn some money…"

Rod interrupted: "Look, spare me the poor-immigrant story. I need to know if you are willing to play ball with us and receive a pass from our government, or are you going to continue to ride the train you're on?"

Katrina sat back in the chair and, at a loss for words and in an expression of innocence, halfway questioned, "What are you saying? Am I now a suspect in a murder? I just helped Mr. Lucas out because he liked me and wanted to provide for me in my time of need."

Rod then in his cynical mode returned with "Yeah, yeah, Lucas, a known drug dealer and criminal boss, in lieu of making his annual donation to St. Jude, decided to provide a home for a sexy, good-looking bitch like you simply because of his charitable nature." He then continued, "Katrina, no offense, darling, but either you think I am the biggest fool in the world or you need to stop and replace all the marbles."

Katrina's good sense began to awaken amid all Rod's criticism and demeaning responses, and with a bit of seriousness in her expression, she then asked Rod, "I have to make all these decisions now?" She then went on with "I, I need to think—I need time to understand what you are saying and what you want me to do."

Rod now, with a touch of compassion, toned it down but in a firm voice said, "Katrina, I do understand where you are coming from. If you are even being honest with me or blatantly kicking me in the balls, I am not sure, but I will give you some time to think about all this before giving me an answer." Rod then finished with "However, I want your answers in two days, by Friday at noon." Rod then questioned, "Where can I find you on Friday?"

Katrina was experiencing anxiety from all the questions. The need to answer whether she would cooperate with the law for possible exoneration from her involvement with a known criminal boss, which was probably a death trap, or remain silent left her in a predicament. She looked hard at Rod and tried to come into focus with what he was asking and replied, "I guess I would be here." She then retracted that and again answered with "No, I don't want you to come here ever again. I want to meet you somewhere that no one will know." She then stated, "I have to think. Give me a place or a phone number to call you."

Rod then wrote down a cell number he had always used for his previous snitches to call and handed it to her. Rod then walked out the door and, without looking back from his tall broad physique, retorted, "Call me!"

CHAPTER 7
THE ESCAPE

The Huntsville prison yard was quiet, and Nicholas was seated on an outdoor bench with one leg cocked up on the edge of the bench as he leaned on his knee, chewing on a piece of straw. The public-address system sounded with an attention blast, as it always did before a forthcoming message. The message this time again was for prisoner Nicholas Musso, number 1509, to report to the assembly station, as again he had a visitor. Nicholas this time was not curious because he expected Victoria to return with further instructions from her father. However, when he arrived in the meeting area, he discovered it was a man of approximately his same height and build waiting at his assigned table. The man was well dressed in a gray flannel suit and a dark blue tie with a white shirt. Nicholas walked up to the table and stared directly at the seated gentleman's eyes and questioned, "And you are?"

The well-dressed man looked up and replied, "Let's say, for argument's sake, I am your attorney, sent by a common friend."

Nicholas, in a curious vein, sat across the table and asked, "Exactly what are you going to legally do for me?"

The individual then glanced to both sides as if to see if anyone was listening and responded, "My employer wants you to know that it will not be long before he comes for you and he wants you to be ready."

Nicholas then wondered what the plan was for his extraction from these prison walls and again questioned, "I am sure your employer has a plan, but I don't know what that plan is and when I should be ready."

The individual then placed both his hands on his own face, in a sense as if to maintain an environment of secrecy, and replied to Nicholas, "That is the purpose of my visit." He then extended his explanation in a low tone. "Look, Mr. Musso, my employer said to tell you that you would know because a surprise visit would be your call to come to the visitors' room without question."

Nicholas, now in total frustration, reiterated, "Look, whoever you are, I was expecting Victoria to come here with a plan or at least some informative instructions for me to follow before any surprise visit happened."

The individual again tried to calm Nicholas as he retorted with "You have to maintain your cool or you are going to fuck this up!"

The man then began to rise from his chair in a motion to depart. Nicholas, with a face full of questions, excitedly stated, "Whoa, wait a minute. I am still at a loss here." He then, in a rant, said, "I mean, I don't even know what it is that he needs me to do."

The man then turned around and with a worried look replied, "You have all the information you need at this point, so relax, because my employer realizes what you know and has a plan." He then finished with "I need to go, and enough has been said." The man then turned and left while Nicholas sat quietly with a total expression of confusion on his face.

Rod, now seated at an Applebee's, was enjoying a burger and a glass of tea when his snitch phone rang.

Katrina, on the other end of the line, immediately began complaining as she vocalized her thoughts to Rod. "Mr. FBI Man, I have been thinking about this for two nights, and I can't sleep." Rod then, in a calm demeanor, answered, "Katrina, slow down and tell me what your biggest concern is in helping us."

Katrina, now taking a line from Rod, responded, "Duh! Dying!" She then pushed further with "Who is going to stop Mr. Lucas from blowing my brains out?"

Rod then countered with "We will protect you, Katrina."

She then, still in a sarcastic tone, answered, "Oh, sure you will, and if you fail and I end up dead you have lost nothing." She then asked, "What assurance do I have?"

Rod, now seeing her as a real possibility because of her extreme concern for her own life, decided he needed to meet with her again and remove her worries to restore her confidence. He then told her, "Katrina, you need to calm down and meet me." He then informed her, "Look, call me back in one hour on this same phone, and I will provide you with a location where we can talk, OK?"

Katrina breathed heavily and replied, "OK."

A quadcopter drone with a mounted video camera slowly approached the Huntsville prison from the west, being monitored from a white van just off Sam Houston Avenue, parked facing north. The two individuals in the van were viewing a flat computer screen illustrating an aerial view of the prison and recording as it approached the perimeter walls. The high buzzing sound of the drone drew the attention of the guards and prisoners as the unit slowed to a halt and hovered above. The guards reported the suspicious drone

THE ESCAPE

to the main office. The warden was then notified and made a quick call to the FBI hotline. Two black official vehicles were deployed immediately from an office in the vicinity. The guards in the tower questioned the main office, "Do we shoot it down?"

The desk office then questioned the warden by phone: "Tower guards are asking if they should blow it out of the sky."

The warden replied, "No, let me have a look—and those two couldn't hit a 747, much less a drone."

Ten minutes passed, and the drone continued to hover and take video as the two official vehicles arrived on the scene. The monitors flew the drone to the north side of the prison as it departed the area. One of the black vehicles then, in an attempt to follow, pulled out and headed west. The drone then returned to the prison, and the warden said, "Shoot it down!" The tower guard took aim with his .30-06 high-powered rifle mounted with a scope, and as the crosshairs zeroed in on the drone, he fired. The drone immediately exploded and disintegrated in midair. The white van along Sam Houston Avenue pulled out and headed north and disappeared.

Rod, sitting across the table, staring at Katrina, in a nondescript tavern located on the east side of Laredo about two blocks over from Mr. Champane's warehouse, where she had first lured him into a trap, questioned, "What will make you feel safe?"

Katrina looked back and retorted, "Ten-foot walls and a vault door."

Rod then, in a cynical tone, questioned, "So you would feel safe in a prison is what you are telling me?"

She then arrogantly replied, "No, you fool, don't you understand? Lucas can get to you anywhere, and he will kill me."

Rod softened and in an effort to destress Katrina then stated, "Look, we will relocate you and provide you with a new identity, and there is no possible way for him to ever get to you." Rod then changed his approach and in a more direct FBI tone relayed to Katrina the existing situation and conditions and then said, "Katrina, the fact is that Gus Lucas is already suspicious of you because he knows you were questioned by us, and the truth is he probably has a plan to take you out." He then finished with "Look what he did with Mr. Champane, a loyal supporter."

Katrina, with a very depressed look, but also with an expression of understanding, then asked, "What will become of me?" and cried, "I have family that I can never see again!"

Rod emphatically responded, "If you are dead, that's pretty definite you won't ever see them again."

Five days had passed, and Victoria Lucas returned to the Huntsville prison. She was now sitting across from Nicholas for a second time, and she even looked more appealing, with her glowing long hair and dressed to catch everyone's eye. She focused directly on him. She explained to him that the time was near and that when the unusual occurred, he needed to be aware and alert because he would be extracted. Nicholas questioned, "How can I be alert if I have no knowledge of the plan?"

Victoria leaned over and whispered in his left ear with a brief explanation, and Nicholas's eyes widened as she ended with "Do not look surprised at this moment, and whatever you do, do not speak

THE ESCAPE

of this." She then added, "Oh, I am reminded to inform you this is only for you and no one else, understand?" Nicholas nodded a yes. "I understand," he said, but he had an expression of complete wonder across his face.

Another four days went by, and the time was nearing 3:00 p.m. when an eighteen-wheeler was traveling south on Highway 75 to the dead-end intersection of Eleventh Street and then turned left and then right on Avenue I and accelerated toward the Huntsville prison's west wall. Nicholas, sitting on a bench against the blockhouse wall, heard the revved-up sound of the approaching truck as it crashed into the perimeter fence and wiped the barbed wire around the cab and continued toward the brick-walled unit. The truck, with doors on both sides swinging open a moment before impact and the driver and passenger jumping to escape, then hit the wall. The cab exploded upon impact with more than a normal such collision would produce. Imploding charges continued to ignite, resulting in mass destruction of the old brick wall and concrete. Flames shot up the wall and also engulfed the eighteen-wheeler, exploding the enclosed trailer and increasing the mass devastation over the extended area. The tower guards were looking for shelter from the flying debris and blinding smoke that continued down within the tower enclosure. Shattered glass, sections of timber framing, and brick and block chips, along with loads of debris, spread across the open prison grounds.

The two escapees, clothed in fire-resistant jumpsuits and helmets that had FBI insignia labeled on each side, rushed in through the enveloping smoke now covering the yard. They knew exactly the location of Nicholas, who was hovering below the bench table he had been seated on earlier, and grabbed him and headed back toward the huge gaping hole in the wall of the prison. The pursuit of the three headed toward the blinking lights of the two awaiting emergency medical service vehicles parked along Avenue I. The back doors of one of the EMS units opened, and two uniformed paramedics assisted the injured prisoner and one FBI agent into the vehicle. Sirens blared, and both EMS units sped away north and turned left on Eleventh Street, then right on Highway 75. The EMS units split up at Highway 1791, where one unit turned left, then south on I-45 toward Houston, while the other unit headed north and merges onto I-45 and continued in a northerly direction toward Dallas. The EMS units with lights flashing were moving quickly in opposite directions while the confusion back at the prison was still unfolding. Guards with weapons in hand were now controlling prisoners away from the explosion area to a section of the prison yard. They were not sure if more was to come as each guard nervously shouted erratically at the convicts in an attempt to maintain order.

Several hours had passed, and sirens from emergency and police units could be heard as the destroyed area was now surrounded by National Guard. The scene at the prison had fire trucks shooting jets of water into the remaining destroyed rubble. A task force of state police had formed a line in the shape of a semicircle, blocking off the possibility of escape from the vulnerable damaged location outside the prison. Firemen in fire-protective clothing scoured the exterior debris. The prison guards continued locking up all the inmates in safe areas. Local FBI senior agent Tim McCally, a fifty-eight-year old, bald-headed, thirty-four-year career specialist was on the scene with a serious expression on his face as he requested to see the video surveillance footage immediately. Timing was important, as he realizes this was a break-in for a tactical escape purpose.

THE ESCAPE

He needed to see the perimeter cameras, as he was also suspicious the extraction vehicles had long since departed and were on a major highway traveling across the state of Texas.

The warden was now broadcasting over the intercom, requesting the guards to take a headcount and report anyone missing. Also, the infirmary had eighteen prisoners and three guards who had been injured in the explosion. The guard reported that two of the prisoners might have to be transported to a burn unit in Dallas, as their burns were extensive. Interesting was the fact that there was no loss of life at this point. Agent McCally, reviewing the video footage, remarked, "This was a well-planned and well-timed explosion, and now we need to know why and where they are." The time continued to click away, and the view on the screen was the eighteen-wheeler approaching the perimeter fencing. The next scene showed the truck crashing into the fence, then the building and the resulting explosion. McCally pushed forward on the video and saw the two EMS units. He immediately called headquarters on his cell and put out a 150-mile-area APB on all highways. The search began with helicopters spanning the Houston area and I-45 north toward Dallas. They found one of the EMS units abandoned just off an exit approximately one hundred miles northeast of Huntsville, with no trace of anyone or any residual from passengers. It wasn't long when a call came in with the exact same scenario just off the I-45 south of Huntsville before entering Houston. Even the fingerprints had been wiped clean. The prison guards were going from cell to cell, checking occupancy in individual units. The bar door to Nicholas's cell slid open, and there, with his leg cocked up on the bed, sat Nicholas, staring, with a piece of straw in his mouth, right at the guards.

CHAPTER 8
THE ARRIVAL

Agent McCally, after researching all possibilities, and in his deductive reasoning, now wanted to know a list of all visitors over the last three months. The APB had been called off because they had no vehicle identification to search for after the abandonment of the EMS units. His thought process was to check with agents in the nearby cities to get a feel for what investigation might have warranted such a break-in. Who were they targeting, and was this a fake deployment or decoy for some other major development forthcoming? In addition, all airports large and small in southeast Texas were being immediately interrogated in an effort to find out what small planes were flown out since the time of the discovery of the abandoned EMS units. McCally was especially interested in the Mexican border towns, because this major style of a break-in into a federal prison was very costly and required heavy financing, so he contacted the Houston office. He knew Brad Kingsworth, the chief agent, and had worked with him previously before being assigned to the Huntsville prison. Brad answered the phone, and McCally in a greeting tone responded, "Brad, how are you? Haven't seen you in a while, and although you are just down the road, we never seem to cross paths."

THE ARRIVAL

Brad, having already heard about the prison break-in, quickly answered, "Well, you got your hands full right now, and I guess this isn't a social call, Tim."

McCally quickly responded, "No, Brad, I have a complex situation and need a little help."

Brad then, in an assisting demeanor, questioned, "What can I do to help you, Tim?" McCally, with an exasperated expression, asked, "Do you have any agents working near the border or any major cases? Because I have a feeling this devastation at Huntsville stinks of cartel money."

Brad's face lit up, as he was well aware of Rod and Troy's ongoing case down in Laredo, and he explained to Tim, "Well, as a matter of fact, I have two agents working on a murder case down in Laredo that involves Gus Lucas, who is a big link in the Mexican cartel life."

McCally then became extremely interested, as this might be the connection he was searching for in both money and a plot. McCally then requested from Brad, "How can I contact Rod?" He continued with "I remember Rod Tillman when he first got into the investigating end, and he was a pretty smart cookie."

Brad answered, "Yes, he's got a lot of street smarts, and if he could only find a box to store that sarcasm in, he's probably one of my best field agents out there." Brad finished with "I tell you what—I will contact Rod because he is in a very complex period of time and may not answer your call, and I will have him call you, OK?"

Tim was OK with that but was anxious to move on his own investigation and gave Brad his contact information and ended with "Brad, please do this for me soon because timing is key in this case."

THE RESOLVE

Brad tactfully said, "Tim, I will take care of it!" Brad realized that Rod was very sensitive when it came to any interference with his ongoing casework.

Rod and Katrina, riding together with a suitcase and a back seat full of her household treasures, were heading north on I-35 to San Antonio, where Rod had booked a room under Troy McGinnis's name at the Hyatt Regency near the River Walk in the downtown area. He had Troy call ahead, as he feared that Lucas and the gang might have already made assumptions utilizing his identity. He explained to Katrina, "Look, we need for you to feel safe and get you away from Laredo and Lucas."

She then questioned, "What about the rest of my stuff?"

Rod replied, "It is best for the moment to leave everything in place as if nothing is going on and you have just taken time to go visit someone."

Katrina became worried, as she now began thinking of her family, most of which lived near Mexico City. She questioned, "Suppose they go looking for my family and hurt them?"

Rod then asked, "Does he know your family and where they live?"

She answered, "No, not really, because I use a fake last name, and that has never come up that I remember."

Rod then, with an eye roll and under his breath, stated, "Thank God for that." He turned to Katrina and with some feeling of confidence told her, "Katrina, you will be fine, and I will have an expert go in like a family friend and make sure you left no information about your family, and we will remove all phone records."

THE ARRIVAL

Katrina, getting the full sense of Rod's very detailed precautionary actions to protect her, softly stated, "I am so very lucky to have you taking care of me."

Rod turned and observed the dreamy look on her face and realized her emotions were now being overcome with a romantic tone.

Rod's cell phone rang, and it was Brad questioning his whereabouts, and Rod replied, "I am resolving a security problem, and I will have to get back to you on that matter."

Brad said, "Well, I need you to call Agent Tim McCally in Huntsville," and then stated, "I guess you heard on the news about the explosive break-in at the Huntsville Unit, and Tim is investigating possibilities connected to your case with Gus Lucas."

Rod, with a concerned look and a small turn toward Katrina, questioned, "Really…That brings on a number of questions in my mind and may have an effect on my pressing security issues. I will call him when I get to a safe line, but can you text me his contact info?"

Brad, with a worried look, tightened his jaw and closed with "Will do."

McCally, waiting to hear from Rod, was now looking over the visitation records at the prison. He did come across the fact that Nicholas Musso, inmate number 1509, had had several recent visitations but also noted he was still accounted for at the prison. His cell phone rang, and it was Brad again, explaining Rod's situation down in Laredo and that he would be sending Tim's contact information to another agent named Troy McGinnis, who was also in Laredo working with Rod. Tim responded with "Well, Brad, you know time is of the essence, and this issue can't wait." He then continued, "I really don't have any missing inmates other than those injured, and all those are accounted for at the infirmary burn unit in Dallas."

Brad countered with "Tim, pay close attention to anyone being transported anywhere, because the guy who planned this is good." Brad paused and reiterated, "He is really good."

A late-model black Lincoln MKS, after making its way from Houston and then through San Antonio, traveled south to Laredo and pulled into a large street garage. The metal doors slid up, and the Lincoln pulled in, and standing with his hands on his hips, belly fat inching over his belt buckle, was Gus Lucas. The final moment of anticipation had arrived, along with his long-awaited guest, who stepped out the back seat of the vehicle. Nicholas Musso looked up as he exited and smiled at Gus and said in a low tone, "Hell, you did it."

Gus, with open arms and a big grin, blurted out, "My friend, I got you back." And then he gave Nicholas a big hug. Nicholas, never being the most affectionate individual one would encounter, and certainly having no appreciation for the Latin cultural gesture of hugging, halfheartedly, with his right arm, returned Gus's greeting as a matter of respect.

Nicholas then responded with a spontaneous feeling of being free as he just took a deep breath and released it. "Whatever it is, man, I am with you!"

Lucas, with a hearty grin, glanced at everyone around and vocalized, "You hear this guy?"

Nicholas had changed his prison garb for the supplied new wardrobe, but he needed a shave and was anxious to clean up and possibly

THE ARRIVAL

get a taste of something different from the ongoing cuisine he had become accustomed to every day. Lucas, with his obvious gangster-style charm oozing out, invited Nicholas to come into an adjacent room with a large table and bowls of food set in place, along with several place settings. Nicholas entered and scanned around the room, this being his habitual reaction from his incarceration. Gus sensed his uneasiness and attempted to calm him and said, "Have a seat. Relax. We are all friends here." He then, in a more serious tone, stated, "We need to eat, get comfortable, and make some plans." Nicholas, with his stomach rumbling, aggressively served himself some black beans and a large steak that appeared fairly well done. He commenced to eat, holding his fork between his thumb joint and forefinger as you would expect from jail-time manners. Gus, leaning back in his chair, sipping on a glass of ice and tequila and not eating, but instead observing his friend, said, "We have a big shipment in Nicaragua that is going to be flown into Monterey and then finally transported here." He stopped and glanced around at his Mexican crew, also seated at the table, and then added, "I need you to help me get it here."

Nicholas stopped chewing, swallowed, and then questioned, "Why me?" He then followed with "You went to big-time trouble to get me here to do this?" He then stared directly at Gus and said, "You have plenty of hombres to do this job—why me?"

Gus, no longer smiling, answered, "Three words why: accountability, trust, and accuracy." He then continued with "I know you are accountable for getting it all here, and I know I can trust you, and most important is the fact that you cover all the details." He ended with "You are a very accurate man."

Nicholas now, being inquisitive, then questioned, "This must be a really big shipment?"

Gus, realizing this would be a natural concern coming from Nicholas, but not wanting to reveal all the cards at this point, especially in front of his big-eared crew, replied with "Well, I went to a lot of trouble and expense to get you here, my friend."

Nicholas, picking up on the fact that Gus was not ready to provide such a revelation at this time, understood why and left it with "I understand." The Mexican crew, looking at each other, were not about to interject in any of the dialogue. The crew members begin to grin at one another but remained silent.

Rod dialed his cell phone, and the voice on the other end was Agent McCally. "Mr. McCally, Agent Rod Tillman. I hear you are looking for me?"

McCally then answered, "Yes, I am, and maybe you don't remember me, but I remember you back when you first began investigations." McCally then quickly inserted, "Look, we can reacquaint another day, but now I have a serious situation really kicking me in the ass, and maybe you can help me."

Rod answered with "Yeah, I heard about it on the news." Rod then reassured him, "Yes indeed, whatever I can do. I am listening."

McCally, now a bit more confident with Rod's willingness to jump in, said, "You see, I am of the strong opinion, due to the extravagance and planning of this breakout or break-in, whatever the hell this was, that the cost narrows this source to drugs!" McCally now, in a high tone, explained, "These drugs, I'm guessing, are funneled here via cartels from Mexico, Colombia, or Nicaragua, and there is a connection at the border." He then added, "Which border town I don't know, but Laredo would fit my guesswork."

THE ARRIVAL

Rod now, with his mind racing with his recent activities with Gus Lucas and the gang, began with "I see the link, along with the possibilities," and then interjected, "Excellent detective work, Mr. McCally, and I am in the middle of a case that would appear to fit in your jailbreak." Rod then ended with "Well, sir, all we have to do now is begin putting the pieces of the puzzle in place."

McCally, biting his bottom lip with the right side of his top teeth, returned in an inquisitive mode, "Yep, all I have to do is determine the reason for the break-in, Mr. Tillman."

Prisoner 1509 now requested of the guard to be allowed to go to the infirmary because he thought his arm was injured from the explosion. The guard responded, "OK, Mr. Musso, we will have a guard bring you to the infirmary in five minutes. Stay in your cell till we come get you." The guard made the request on his shoulder intercom and shortly thereafter escorted prisoner 1509 to the infirmary. Two white-uniformed guards chained him to a gurney in an exam room to await the physician on call for the prison. Approximately thirty minutes passed, and a male nurse technician entered with a clipboard in hand and questioned his injury. Prisoner 1509 went into detail about how the pain in his right side and right arm from the explosion was debilitating him and growing increasingly worse. The technician reported back to the doctor, and the doctor ordered an x-ray of his right side. When the technician returned to take prisoner 1509 to x-ray, as he released the handcuff chain with his universal key, 1509 grabbed him with the chain and utilized his other hand over his mouth to maintain silence and strangled him with the chain. The technician began to slip from his arms, and 1509 grabbed the key to free himself from the chains. Prisoner 1509 then turned to the reflection in the side glass and ripped off the intricately formulated skin of the facial mask disguise and revealed his true identity as the male visitor who had come to see Nicholas Musso earlier. He then removed the tech's uniform and badge from the technician on the floor and exchanged his prison jumpsuit, as they were close in stature. He next dragged the technician and lifted him into a laundry bin that he pulled in from outside the exam room door. He next walked to the door to the guard station, shined his badge, and walked toward the front administrative section. No one seemed to be concerned as 1509 exited the prison to the front street and a gray pickup truck drove up, and he jumped in, and they drove off.

Rod was trying to correlate the prison breakout and the cartel's possible connection. He sat back in his chair and flipped a pencil back and forth with his fingers. He knew he needed to figure this out before McCally. He decided to call Brad back and pushed his cell phone button. Brad answered, "Yes, Rod?"

Rod then questioned, "Did McCally happen to mention a particular escapee or any missing prisoners?"

Brad then, with a humdrum expression, replies, "Well, no, but that is exactly what he is trying to determine."

Rod then emphatically said, "You can bet your tight wallet, Brad, that it won't be long before that becomes apparent!" Rod hung up and with an earnest look stated to himself, "I might have to go to Huntsville."

CHAPTER 9
THE PICKUP

The six o'clock buzzer sounded in the prison, relating to all the guards to line up their cellblocks for the evening inmate chow line. The guard that had brought 1509 to the infirmary realized he had not been returned. He went to the infirmary and questioned his condition, and no one seemed to be sure of his whereabouts. An immediate search in the x-ray room and the holding cell resulted in no discovery of the prisoner. The technicians, being very cognizant of prisoner attempts to hide in garment buggies, began searching each one and found the assigned technician strangled among the covered blue scrubs. The alarm sounded in the prison, and the search began with an aggressive investigation by all the guards. Agent Tim McCally immediately went to the monitors to review the cameras to detect if anyone departed in a technician's scrubs from the prison. He saw Musso's clone's departure and the gray pickup truck driving up and then departing. McCally requested the programmer to blow up the license plate and then put it out in an all-points bulletin to all the sheriffs' offices in the areas around Huntsville. His mind began to seek a plot that was missing. He then returned to the visitors' log and reviewed dates and times. He noted that a woman had visited several weeks prior and then recently again. The identity shown was an obvious fake, but the picture was clear. He reviewed the cameras to get a closer visual of the woman and the male visitor who was also on the list. Utilizing the videos, he expanded the search through the FBI files for an identity.

—⁂—

Gus Lucas stood next to a six-seat Cessna 206 twin-engine airplane on a grass strip just north of Laredo with Nicholas as the pilot cranked up the turboprops and a whiff of smoke blew in the wind. Gus looked directly at Nicholas and emphasized, "You know what to do, my friend," and then added, "I have faith in you." Nicholas boarded the plane, and the engines now revved up as the pilot positioned the Cessna toward the open runway. The engines reached a high shrill, and the plane began the approach and streamed down the graded, smooth grass strip until it lifted and flew to the south. Lucas remained standing at the site with the rush of wind flapping the edge of his sports coat while he stared at the plane's liftoff. His face had a stern expression and almost a look of suspicion about his old friend's involvement.

—⁂—

Rod and Katrina, now at a table in the café adjacent to the Hyatt Regency in San Antonio, each sipping a cup of coffee and Katrina nibbling on a muffin, were quiet for the moment. Rod stared at Katrina's big brown eyes and smooth complexion as she looked at him with a dependent expression on her face. The sense of security he was now emanating brought on a lure of affection, and she reached across the table, grabbing his hand, and softly said, "I need you now, Mr. FBI Man."

Rod, realizing the sexual connotation, had a big decision to make on whether he conceded to her special needs or risked losing her support in this case. Having sex with a material witness in a possible major crime is extremely dangerous in so many ways. However, Rod, now lying next to Katrina in the hotel room, explained to her, "You know this is completely out of the rule book and my career is in jeopardy, with your hand on the throttle?"

She responded, "You have nothing to fear. I am in your hands all the way." She continued, "I have taken the steps to get out, and I need you to keep me safe."

Rod then, in an assuring tone, replied, "I will—just do what I tell you and do not hesitate." Rod, feeling confident that this all remained secure with her intense need of his support, rendered a quirky smile as if to say, "I made the right move!"

Troy McGinnis now called Rod on his cell phone, and as Rod answered with "Yes,"Troy responded, "Where the hell are you, man?"

Rod, in a calm demeanor, responded, "I am making sure the witness is secure, and you know that."

Troy then complained, "I have my thoughts about your security measures, but things are beginning to bubble back here in Laredo."

Rod questioned, "What's going on?" Troy, in an expression of anxiety, then stated, "Well, that agent Tim McCally at the Houston prison sent two of his agents here to investigate that break-in, and they are looking for you."

Rod then, frustrated, asked, "What did you tell them?" and then again questioned Troy: "You didn't tell them where I am?"

Troy, in a "Don't you trust me?" tone, replied, "Of course not. I know better than that. Have a little faith." Troy then, worried, asked, "Well, Rod, what do I tell them?"

THE RESOLVE

Rod, concerned about these agents, then explained, "Troy, you tell them I am on another assignment. As I told their boss, I will get back to them when I have something." Rod then suspiciously added, "Also question them for details on exactly what they are looking for here in Laredo." Rod then pushed the off button on his phone, looked at Katrina sitting up in the bed, a naked beauty with the sheet partially draped over her, and began to ponder a method to check out these two agents.

Nicholas was staring out the window of the Cessna as they glided over the hilltops of Nicaragua at a fairly low altitude to avoid any major radar attractions that might be located in the area. He questioned the pilot, who had been mostly silent throughout the flight, "Señor, how much longer before we land?"

The pilot then turned and looked at Nicholas with a matter-of-fact look on his face and replied, "Fifteen minutes, or maybe less." Nicholas, not knowing who he was supposed to meet when they landed, became somewhat anxious and questioned the pilot once again, asking, "Do you know who we are to meet once we land?"

The pilot then answered, "Si, Señor, a Mr. Miguel Esquivez. He will drive you to the warehouse in San Carlos." The pilot, who obviously knew more than Nicholas, elaborated, "Señor Lucas says you are de boss, and we will make the first load in the plane and then return three more times because of de weight."

Nicholas, now getting the picture, became increasingly concerned over being caught by the feds or being blown up possibly by cartel activists in an attempt to curb Gus Lucas and his operations.

THE PICKUP

He then questioned the pilot, "Who else knows about this pickup and delivery system?"

The pilot then responded with a somewhat softer voice, "Señor, we keep this very quiet because Señor Lucas would…" He pulled his index fingers across his throat in a direct means to demonstrate that Gus Lucas would have them killed if they were to expose his plan. Nicholas then puckered his lips and shook his head in a yes motion, and his eyes rolled upward, acknowledging that he understood.

Rod was now back on the cell phone, calling Tim McCally at the Huntsville prison. McCally, seeing it was Rod Tillman on the ID of his phone, answered, "McCally here!"

Rod then asked, "Tim, who are the two agents you sent to Laredo on the break-in case?" McCally, somewhat bewildered, then responded with "Well, Rod, I haven't sent any agents to Laredo as of this time."

Rod's suspicions were now coming to reality, and he then decides he didn't want to let on that he knew that these agents were bogus. He then explained to Tim, "Look, whoever these guys are, they are attempting to investigate the case I have ongoing, which I think is connected with your break-in, so for now can we keep this totally under the sheets until I find out who is behind their inquiries?"

Tim, understanding Rod's reasons for keeping this under wraps but still concerned about the two agents using his name, stated to Rod, "You got it, friend, but you will, when you can, let me know who these unknown undercover agents are and the reasons for their inquiries, agreed?"

Rod then answered, "I will as soon as I get to the bottom of this garbage."

Rod, now driving back toward Laredo, then called Troy back and in a suspicious tone explained to him, "Look, Troy, I am not sure who these agents are, so let's do a little undercover interrogation ourselves, OK?"

Troy, shaking his head with a yes profile as a gesture of understanding, replied to Rod, "I got you, good buddy. Sounds like a plan to me."

Rod then requested, "Look, Troy, I know it is late, but I think I am in for a possible surprise, and I need you to come to my hotel room and hang around for a while to see if our guests show up. Follow?"

Troy again responded, "Got it!"

In the dark of night, Rod arrived in Laredo and headed to the Residence Inn. He slipped his key in and opened the door to his room, walked in, and sat on the bed. His eyes stared straight ahead, and he allowed his thoughts to ponder. He pulled his gun from the shoulder holster, checked the clip for bullets, and then leaned against the headboard. Three hours had passed. and Rod now, in the dark, was standing just inside the bathroom doorway with his gun cocked and positioned next to his cheekbone as he heard the shuffling sound at his hotel room door. The door carefully began to open. The glare from the corridor provided sufficient light to enhance the silhouette of two tall, heavyset men entering the room with weapons grasped in a position to fire. They were both holding 9-millimeters with silencers attached. Upon them both being fully within the foyer of the room and the door closed, Rod placed his gun at the base of the neck of the second man. The first man turned as he heard the rustling behind him and Troy, inside the room, appeared with his gun placed on the temple of the first perpetrator. Rod then demanded, "Either put them down or be the victims!"

Both individuals dropped their weapons, and Rod and Troy pushed them against the wall and cuffed them. Rod then walked around both men, who were now lying face down on the floor in the middle of the room as the leader of the two attempted an explanation when he grunted out, "Look, we are Secret Service agents just doing our job!"

Rod replied in a sarcastic vein, "Yes, and I am Elmer Fudd looking for 'wabbits.'" Rod continued, "I can't wait to hear why you came in with guns with silencers cocked and ready, FBI issue?" Both men had "How do we explain this?" looks on their faces and were trying another round of explanation when Rod interrupted, "And exactly who is it you were preparing to defend yourselves from—or I should say 'take out with your undercover intrusion'?"

The leader, at a loss for words, then stated, "We are undercover and cannot talk about the case."

Troy, having been quiet in his own cynical way, then spoke as he apparently rolled his eyes: "Don't the bad guys have any smarter hired hands than you two?" Troy then finished with "I mean, we are FBI, and you think we'll fall for this line of bullshit?"

Rod then began to pull them up to a standing position and told Troy, "Let's get these two geniuses to the station, and they can finish telling us this fantasy story down there." Rod then asked Troy, "Are the patrol units here?" He then put his gun to the leader's head and demanded to him "Please, make a move and give me a reason to waste you" as they headed out the door.

THE RESOLVE

While Troy pushed the head of the second man down into the local patrol unit, Rod was on his cell. He was waiting for Tim McCally to answer. McCally answered with anticipation: "Tillman, you got something for me?"

Rod then informed him, "Yes, and these guys are obviously no agents, but I do think they are connected somehow to this whole thing."

McCally then responded, "See what you can find out. I may take a ride down there to ask a few of my own questions."

Rod responded, "Will do, Chief, but first let us interrogate them and see if we can't find out who the head honchos are giving them their direction."

Nicholas, now standing next to the plane on a private grass strip just outside the metropolis of San Carlos, Nicaragua, scanned the area, searching for possible abnormal intrusions by either opponents of Lucas or law enforcement. The pilot then came up to him and stated, "Señor, a man in a truck will be coming to pick you up, and I will wait here wit' da plane." Nicholas nodded, without looking at him, in a "yes" gesture.

Moments later, what appeared to be an old-model Chevy truck pulled up in front of the two men and stopped with a squeak. The driver, a Latino man, stuck his head out the window and questioned Nicholas: "You are Señor Nicholas, the boss man?"

Nicholas, with an unsure expression on his face, replied to the Latino, "I guess that would be me." Nicholas then walked to the other side of the old truck and got in and then questioned the driver: "The warehouse, is it far from this airstrip?"

THE PICKUP

The driver then, as he pulled out in a cloud of dust, responded, "No, Señor, just a few minutes up the road." Nicholas then informed the driver that he had a broken headlamp on the right side of the truck. The Latino answered, "I know, Señor," as he turned toward Nicholas with a more reassuring look on his face. Nicholas, with a half smile while his expression remained fully in a suspicious mode, grunted and then stared ahead.

CHAPTER 10
THE DECOY

Nicholas and the Latino drove up to a wooded area and down a rock-bed trail that led to an eight-foot-high chain-link fence with barbed wire coiled along the top edge. Although not a foolproof security measure, it was an obvious deterrent for anyone approaching the compound. The compound included two metal buildings that appeared to be warehouses due to the fact there were no obvious windows. The two guards at the gate opened the two large double swinging chain-link leaves and allowed the beat-up old pickup through as if they were expecting him. Nicholas observed the two guards in military fatigues and armed with military automatic rifles. The Latino pulled up and backed up to a wide pull-up-type door on the back side of the warehouse, where three vans with tinted windows and side panels were parked and a stretched long black limousine SUV was also parked alongside. The driver jumped out of the pickup and headed to a side door, opened it, and turned to face Nicholas, who was still seated in the vehicle, observing the surroundings. Nicholas then retreated slowly from the truck and headed toward the opened door and entered.

Nicholas, as he walked up, was frisked from head to toe for a possible weapon. He immediately turned with an angry demeanor and faced a small-framed Filipino dressed in a coat and tie, with horn-rimmed brass round glasses mounted on his face. The Filipino faced Nicholas and greeted him formally with "Hello, Mr. Musso. I am Ed, Mr. Lucas's manager of this facility." As Nicholas surveyed the room, he saw thirty or more dark-haired Spanish-looking women with plastic shower caps on their heads and masks across their noses and mouths standing completely nude at bench tables. They were filling bags with the white powder. Mr. Ed then, after a short pause, responded, "I'm sorry for this body search, but we are never sure the right person is entering our factory."

Nicholas, now understanding the Filipino's reckoning, took on a calm appearance and interjected, "I guess you can't be too secure." He then added, "How did you know that was the right truck entering the gate?"

The Filipino immediately answered, "We broke the right headlight."

Tim McCally, now facing Troy across the desk at the local station headquarters, stated, "I had to come and see for myself who are you dealing with and what the hell is going on."

Troy then answered, "Agent McCally, what we are able to piece together is that this whole case follows a leader named Gus Lucas." Troy then continued, "Gus Lucas is a come-up-through-the-ranks leader of a South American cartel and made his home base somewhere in Nicaragua or some nearby Central American country." He then stated, "He obviously teamed up with a fellow named Paul Champane from Dallas, as he uses a warehouse that was owned by Mr. Champane in Laredo." Troy then finished with "I don't know why he needed this guy in the Huntsville Unit, but he desperately wanted him out, and that's where you come in, Agent McCally."

Tim, now with a very puzzled look on his face, then spoke up: "I got to tell you, Agent McGinnis, that is quite a story, and so where do we go from here?"

Troy responded, "Well, Rod has an involved woman, somehow connected, agreeing to testify. She is hidden away in a secure location until he can get back to her. Then these two suspicious agents of yours arrived on the scene." He then followed with "Rod and I, not being fooled by their conspicuous false identities, tricked them as to where our witness was being held, and they fell for it like a moth to a light" as he smiles with an air of FBI confidence.

Rod, now questioning the two false agents in interrogation chambers, asked, "I guess you two fools are not going to tell me who is behind your charade because you fear for your lives, right?" He then stated with an affirmed look on his face, "The truth is, I already know that Gus Lucas sent you." The two individuals then looked at each other in disgust that they were intercepted and fell for the trap. They knew Lucas was going to be very unhappy with their capture, and now their lives here on earth were uncertain. Rod followed with "I detect your uneasiness as you try to decide whether you should cough it up or remain silent here in this safe zone, but I can assure you that as you are placed in a cell with other inmates, you become quite vulnerable to the hand of Gus Lucas." Rod then continued with "On the other hand, I am willing to make a deal in reference to your safety depending on what you have to offer." He then began to rise from the table and left with a parting remark—"I will let you two talk it over. I'll be back"—and closed the door behind him. He well knew the chamber had clear audible microphones situated under the table.

Nicholas now followed Ed to a desk with a chair facing Ed and took his seat. Ed then asked Nicholas, "You are obviously aware of your mission, and we are here to assist you in any way you may deem necessary." Nicholas, in a somewhat matter-of-fact mannerism and with a hint of sarcasm, responded, "Well, I guess you are aware of your mission also, so a whole lot of conversation isn't necessary?"

Ed, now a bit set back by Nicholas's whole demeanor, then stated, "I now see why Mr. Lucas picked someone like you, Mr. Musso. You are a man of few words and ready to get the job done!" Ed then continued, "Well, let's fill up the plane and get you on your way." Ed then stood and extended his hand to shake Nicholas's hand, but Nicholas looked at him with an unconvinced look, then turned and headed to the door.

Nicholas was escorted back to the pickup truck, and the white powder was now loaded and covered with a tarp. The Latino, Miguel, seated behind the wheel with an anxious look, was obviously ready to go. Nicholas climbed in, and they drove off through the gate and headed back to the plane. Upon approaching the airstrip, Nicholas then noticed another Cessna 206, which had striping and colors that matched the plane he had arrived in, standing by with the prop turning. Nicholas, becoming weary, questioned Miguel: "Why is that plane next to ours parked there?"

Miguel replied, "Señor, that is our decoy."

"Decoy?" Nicholas asked, as he now had a look of concern. He then mumbled under his breath to the Latino, "Why would we need a decoy unless someone is going to be following us?" They pulled up next to the plane they had arrived in, and the pilot and Miguel immediately began loading the plane with the packaged cargo. Nicholas, standing with his arms folded, leaning against the truck door, continued to stare at the other plane and observe the pilot, another Latin, who stared back at Nicholas.

The plane was now loaded to the max. The pilot, then climbing aboard, exclaimed to Nicholas, "Time to go, Señor." Nicholas also boarded the passenger side of the plane as the engines roared and a puff of exhaust smoke blew in the wind. Nicholas was still eyeing the second plane as that pilot revved up the engine and slowly pulled up in front of Nicholas and the cargo. The second plane sped down the airstrip and glided upward and banked to the right. The pilot and Nicholas followed right behind and flew upward and banked also to the right in the same pattern.

—⁂—

Rod returned to the room with the two fake undercover agents and asked, "Gentlemen, are we ready to talk and possibly save your lives?" The two men looked at each other and then faced Rod, waiting for the other to speak first, resulting in neither saying anything until Rod tilted his head and questioned, "Well, ladies, let's not be shy. One of you obviously wants to tell me something, right?"

The one on the left finally spoke up and stuttered with "You ask, ah, ah, want something from us, but what assurances do we have?"

Rod, seeing the difficulty developing in either of these two being forthcoming, decided to play the I-don't-give-a-damn attitude and quickly retorted with "Up until a minute after I came through that door, you had an opportunity to be safely incarcerated far away

THE DECOY

in a secluded location that Gus Lucas could never find!" Rod then finished with "But now that's gone, and we will begin the process of booking you until trial for attempted murder and just see where it goes."

The second one, on the right, now in desperation blurted out, "OK, OK, we are ready to make a deal!"

Rod paused and then, raising his right eye and wrinkling his brow, asked, "Well, for discussion's sake, let's hear what you have to offer in this deal?"

The second man spoke again and stated, "OK, you got us on breaking and entering with intent, but you don't know if we were going to kill anyone because we were sent to kidnap the informant and bring her to our boss. If we open up to you and tell you everything, we want some immunity and witness protection." The two looked at each other and shook their heads in a "yes" fashion, with both in agreement.

Rod, looking at both of them with a sense that this was a well-thought-out response from two goons, then responded, "That's fine, and I must say I am impressed with your save-your-ass thinking; however, we have to check your records and see what the history books tell us." He then ended with "I will get back to you." He then left the room for a second time.

Nicholas was still staring out of the plane as the pilot veered off to the left and was now on a course directly for Laredo, Texas, across the border. The second decoy plane continued on course for Nuevo Laredo, Mexico, across the border from Laredo. The decoy plane began its descent toward a small airport in Nuevo Laredo. The pilot aligned the plane with the runway and began the descent rapidly. At approximately four thousand feet, the pilot ejected and parachuted a safe distance from the airport. When the plane reached two thousand feet above the ground, before reaching the landing strip, a plastic tube was aimed. That cap flipped open, and the M72 light antiweapon (LAW) missile was fired. The plane exploded above and approximately one quarter mile from the airport. The plane was totally obliterated.

Nicholas, continuing on his flight, heard the boom sound behind him and attempted to turn and see what that was all about. He questioned the pilot, "Did you hear that?" and the pilot looked at him and questioned, "Hear what, Señor?"

Nicholas then, with a deep suspicion, again inquired, "That explosion behind us." Nicholas then, with a concerned tone, professed, "You act dumb, but I think you know more than what you are telling me."

The pilot, in a nervous tone, reacted with a shrugged shoulder and murmured, "Señor, I don't know what you are asking me. I just follow orders, and my boss pays me."

Nicholas, still not feeling real comfortable, returned, with a look of frustration, "I don't like people fucking with me, and I get extremely pissed when I think I am being screwed and I don't know where or when it is coming." Nicholas finished with "I will put a bullet in your head if it turns out you have fucked me—*comprende*, Señor pilot?" The pilot, totally understanding Nicholas's meaning and frustration with all the unknowns, looked straight ahead and continued with his focus on the flight. He knew Gus Lucas would have him eliminated if anything went wrong, as *mucho* money was spent on this mission.

CHAPTER 11
ROMANCE BEGINS

Brad Kingsworth back in Houston got word from the FAA that a plane had exploded over the airport in Nuevo Laredo. He then contacted Rod and expressed his curious concerns as he informed him, "Rod, I got word through the FAA of a small plane blowing up in Nuevo Laredo just south of your location." He then followed with "I don't know if there is any connection to your case with Gus Lucas, but maybe another cartel is sending him a message."

Rod, thinking about the probabilities, responded, "Yes, I get your point, but then again maybe we are all being played in this very involved charade by Mr. Lucas." Rod then closed with "I think I may be getting closer with these two clowns Lucas hired to take out Ms. Katrina."

Brad ended with "Keep me informed, Rod."

Rod then returned to the two henchmen and attempted to bribe them into a confession without a complete release pardon, as he knew neither the district attorney nor the FBI was going to agree to such leniency at this stage of the investigation. He opened the door and stared at the two, who now had a look of some satisfaction that they had made a deal. Rod then proceeded to explain, "Gentlemen, we can't make any deals with you because you have only given us hearsay and nothing for us to consider." He then tightened his lip with a half smile and in a low tone exclaimed, "We simply have no facts!" The two forlorn gangsters' look of hope turned to a look of total frustration. Rod then came forth with a spark of possible light as he puckered his lips and in a tone of solution said, "You know, you are going to have to show us some cooperation for us to consider any possible pleas on your behalf."

Nicholas was now in deep thought and focusing straight ahead as the pilot began his descent to a small airstrip just outside of Laredo, Texas, just north of the Mexican border. The plane was previously cleared through customs, but the reentry to a private airstrip did raise red flags, as several radio transmissions were incoming and the pilot responded. Immigration and Customs was on alert, awaiting the landing and clearance transmissions. The pilot landed the plane, and two agents, upon completion of filling out paperwork, then proceeded toward the plane. One of the officers received a cell call and stopped and answered. He shook his head in an expression of understanding, then motioned to the other agent, and they turned and departed.

Nicholas turned to the pilot and said, "Well, that was interesting. Now what?" Immediately a shiny Navigator SUV drove up, and two dark-haired men in blue jumpsuit uniforms and baseball caps got out and waited for Nicholas and the pilot to depart the plane. Upon the two stepping out, the uniformed men unloaded the plane into the van, and all four left the airstrip, headed to Laredo. Nicholas, still in a suspicious mode, stared at the crew and the pilot and finally broke the silence and questioned, "OK, so where are we headed?"

ROMANCE BEGINS

The pilot quickly responded, "To the warehouse, Señor."

As Nicholas was about to ask another question, two police units with lights flashing and the sirens with quick, pulsing wail sounds blaring pulled up in front and to the rear of the SUV. The police officers retreated from the vehicle with their weapons drawn. The SUV was now at a full stop, and the police, speaking through a megaphone, ordered the occupants to evacuate the vehicle with their hands behind their heads.

All the men, including Nicholas, got out with their hands clasped behind their heads. One of the officers walked up to Nicholas and looked him directly in the face and questioned, "Are you Nicholas Musso?"

Nicholas, realizing there was no alternative and he was caught, replied, "Obviously, you know that." The officer cuffed only Nicholas with his hands to the rear and escorted him to the patrol unit and assisted him into the rear seat. The two police vehicles pulled away, leaving the SUV with the three remaining occupants and the cargo behind. Nicholas, now confused and worried about the unusual and very suspect arrest, stared at the two officers with a squint in his eyes. The vehicle continued on into Laredo and downtown and finally reached a familiar section of the city and stopped in front of a garage door. The door slid up, and both police units pulled into the garage. Nicholas recognized the warehouse as where he was first brought from prison to meet Gus Lucas. The officers stepped out of their respective vehicles and the same one who had questioned Nicholas walked up to him and uncuffed him. Gus Lucas, with his back to Nicholas, turned and looked at him and in a very dry but menacing tone of voice stated, "You passed the test, and now you are ready for the big one!"

THE RESOLVE

Rod returned a second time to the room where the two gangsters were waiting, only on this occasion he was accompanied with two armed agents. He opened the door, and as the two anxious perpetrators tried to still argue their misinterpreted arrest, he ordered the agents to march them to a cell. He informed them, "I am going to give you guys some time to think about your short futures if we don't accept any of your deals and you continue your total lack of cooperation." He finished the conversation with a wave of his hand and stated, "Off we go, boys!" Rod then headed to the exit and out the door, across the street, where he got into his vehicle and drove away. Rod drove toward I-35 but became aware of a suspect late-model black Dodge with two occupants following him through two intersections. He made a turn and traveled three blocks and waited and the same vehicle approached rapidly from the rear. The passenger window slid down and a rifle barrel appeared, shooting off numerous rounds at Rod as the vehicle accelerated toward him. Rod ducked into a low profile on his front seat. The Dodge skated by, sideswiping Rod's vehicle, with bullets penetrating the door and breaking the windshield. Rod immediately rose, not wounded, and stepped on the accelerator in an effort to chase the Dodge. He caught up to them and pulled his 9-millimeter from his shoulder holster and fired five shots into the rear window of the Dodge, shattering the glass. The Dodge made a sharp right and headed down a heavily vehicle-parked street, and Rod continued the chase. The Dodge ran through a red light and was hit by an oncoming utility truck. Both the occupants were killed from the impact. Rod opened his door and, as the shattered

ROMANCE BEGINS

glass fell from the door and his black sports coat, retreated from his vehicle to observe the crash. He noted the personalized license plate with the two words "DEAD MAN." He then mumbled in a low tone, "This shouldn't be hard to trace."

The secure cell phone buzzed on the side table where Katrina sat impatiently waiting to hear from Rod. She immediately grabbed the phone as the potato chip bag fell from her lap onto the bedding and chips fell out. She, in an excited voice, exclaimed, "Where the hell are you? I have been waiting here for two days."

Rod answered with "I got detained on my way to see you; I will be there as soon as I get another car." He then added, "I will be there tonight, and I will take you somewhere safe to have dinner." He concluded with "Be patient" and hung up.

Katrina jumped up from the bed and went into the bathroom, stared into the mirror, and turned her cheek with an under-her-breath remark: "What shall I wear for Mr. FBI Man?"

―⋙―

Nicholas and Gus Lucas were now sitting at a table staring at each other first, and then, without a word, they retreated to looking at a large map displayed on the table. Gus began with "Mr. Musso, this is where you will earn your worth."

Nicholas responded with "Maybe I wasn't that uncomfortable in prison."

Gus immediately responded with a semichuckle: "Yes, Mr. Musso, but at the end of this road, you may be sitting on a sand beach with a beautiful woman and not a worry in the world."

Nicholas answered, "I don't like the beach, and I always worry!" They then both, with pensive looks, began to study the map. Gus pointed to a location near Colombia, South America, and informed Nicholas, "This is where we will load the boat." Then, with a pencil, he drew a line to Mobile, Alabama, and finished with "And this is where we will unload the boat."

Nicholas, somewhat perplexed by Gus and his simplicity in describing the plan, questioned, "And you think that is going to be that easy?" Nicholas continued, "What about the customs agents and all the feds looking for this type of dry smuggling activity now going on?" Nicholas then finished with "What protection do you have in mind?"

Gus then answered with a sarcastic tone, "Mr. Musso, I am disappointed in you. Have you not learned anything in this latest operation of mine, that I plan everything, every detail?" Gus rolled his eyes and up and to the side and exclaimed, "Man, why do you doubt me? Did I not strategically get you out of prison in a well-planned and controlled method of extraction?" Gus concluded with "Have a little faith, Mr. Musso!"

Rod then pulled up to the Hyatt Regency in San Antonio as the dark of night and lights of the street and local businesses now provided a glittered environment. Rod then retreated from the elevator and knocked on the room door. Katrina, although expecting Rod, questioned, "Who's there?" and Rod replied with a hint of humorous sarcasm, "The big bad wolf!"

Katrina opened the door immediately and grabbed him with a big hug and exclaimed, "My God, I am glad to see you!" She was decked out from head to toe with a short, tight skirt and blouse, red lips, heavy eyeshadow, and dangling hooped earrings.

Rod, now aroused, entertained a sexual alternative to dinner but tried to remain professional and in a short tone questioned, "Are you ready for dinner?"

Katrina sensed the sensual inflection and grabbed Rod by the tie and pulled him into the room as she murmured, "We can eat later."

Nicholas now headed out of the warehouse with two other associates of Gus Lucas, both with shaved heads and muscular builds. They got into a black sedan across the street. A driver of Mexican descent pulled the vehicle away from the curb, and Nicholas, staring at the two associates in the back seat, remarked, "Are you two in for the long haul?" They remained silent. The driver, after forty-five minutes, pulled back into the same airstrip where they had arrived earlier. The plane awaiting them was another Cessna 206 twin-engine, but not the one they had arrived in, as the striping colors were different. The engines on the plane were running, and the pilot sat patiently awaiting their arrival. All three men got out of the vehicle and boarded the plane. The pilot revved the engines and aligned the plane for takeoff along the runway. The plane and passengers then departed and headed southward.

Rod sat up in bed in the hotel room and responded, "We got to stop this!" Then, in a few minutes, he and Katrina walked out of the room and got into his vehicle out on the street. They drove to a secluded, hole-in-the-wall small restaurant, and the maître d' at the entrance escorted them to a table in the rear.

They sat down, and Katrina in a sheepish voice questioned Rod, "Am I making you nervous, Mr. FBI Man?" Rod then immediately responded, "I think it is time to bury the 'Mr. FBI Man.'" He then stated, "You can call me Rod when it is just the two of us and Mr. Tillman in the presence of others."

Katrina then smiled and leaned toward him and quietly expressed, "Rod it is! Mr. Tillman!"

Rod smiled back and murmured, "I guess we are both under a degree of pressure, considering the circumstances."

Then, with a sensual look and half smile, Katrina questioned, "Can I have a drink?" Rod continued to observe Katrina and admire her beauty but then realized the extremely serious position he had now placed her in and needed her attention. He looked down at the table and then up and attempted to appeal to her sense of security as he related, "Katrina you have to understand the danger that both you and I are facing."

Katrina, now with an expression of fear, bit her bottom lip and responded, "Rod, now you are really scaring me!"

Rod immediately answered, "That is good Katrina. You need to be scared." He then ended with "These are very serious criminals and will kill you at a moment's notice."

CHAPTER 12
THE ASSAULT

Brad Kingsworth, now sitting at his desk back at headquarters in Houston, had a very upsetting look on his face as he dialed Rod's cell phone. Rod answered quickly, "Brad, it's me."

Brad began immediately with his venting of his frustration. "Rod, when the hell are you going to notify me of what's going on?" He then continued before Rod had a chance to speak: "I got a break-in or breakout, whatever you want to call it, in Huntsville; I got a dead businessman in a warehouse no one can explain; I got a material witness with an attempt on her life…"

Rod then interrupted, "OK, boss, I hear you." Rod then after a short pause reiterated, "I hear you, and I will bring you up to date!" He then, in a last-ditch effort to get a little more time, said "I got those two clowns in custody in Laredo at the local precinct, and I think one of them is about to break!" He finished with "I need one more day to put a package together, and then I will call you."

Brad, in an irritated tone, responded, "Rod, I better hear from you tomorrow!"

Nicholas and his two backup associates were still staring at each other as they were now flying along the east coast of Central America toward Colombia. Nicholas, in an attempt to introduce a dialogue between him and the two muscle supports provided by Gus Lucas, asked, "Did either of you pick up food for this trip?" The two looked at each other in an expression as if to say "What is he talking about?" Nicholas, with a roll of his eyes, stated, "It's amazing that your expressions answer all my questions."

Then the pilot, listening to the conversation, told Nicholas, "Señor Nicholas, there is a cooler in the rear of the plane behind the seats with food and drinks that Señor Lucas put there for us all." Nicholas unbuckled his seat belt and leaned behind the rear seats to extract the cooler contents. The two muscle assistants, now comprehending Nicholas's food concern, looked at each other and begin to chuckle. Nicholas shook his head and expressed his inner thoughts in a condescending voice: "Really, Gus, what were you thinking, putting me out here on such a mission with these two morons?" Nicholas then stared at them and smiled.

Troy was now back in the interrogation room with the two captured perpetrators when Rod walked in the door. Troy looked up at him and greeted him with "Glad to have you back, Rod."

Rod then, with a look of question, glared at the two men sitting at the table and asked, "Well, have you guys thought it over? This is your last chance to talk to us."

The one on the left then hesitantly explained, "We know that you got us on breaking and entering, but you can't convict us on anything else just based on what you think our intentions were!"

Rod thought for a moment and realized that this man did have an excellent chance of being released. He decided to play his previous "ace card" again and then, in a confident voice, as his expression became serious, told them, "OK, you got me, but...what if we let you go and put out the word that we made a deal and we released you." He then added, "You think that ole Gus would believe you or us?" He then finished with "You just have to make the decision whether or not you want to take that risk."

The two looked at each other in silence with very pensive expressions of worry. They together began spilling the beans and explaining what they knew, which was limited, but it confirmed that Gus Lucas was involved. Rod convinced the locals to put out an APB on Mr. Lucas.

The Cessna glided in and landed at a remote airstrip in Colombia. The plane pulled up to a metal warehouse, again with no windows. The plane slowly taxied up to the big roll-up door, which was open, and pulled right on into the building, and the door closed. Nicholas, the two "goons," and the pilot all exited the plane. A gentleman of Spanish descent and wearing a sports coat over a white wrinkled shirt with an open collar approached them, smiling and bright eyed. He looked at Nicholas and said, "Welcome to Colombia, my friends." Nicholas, well aware of the underlying ongoing act and insincerity of these associates of Lucas, returned the look with an under-the-breath grunt. The gentleman then introduced himself. "I am Carlos Montolon, and yes, many confuse my name with the old actor's, but it is not spelled the same." Nicholas realized it didn't matter what names they used, and who cared what anonymity one portrayed in South America, a country ridden with drugs and cartels? Nicholas scanned the open floor of the warehouse and saw nothing stacked ready for shipment but also observed that their present location was only the front of this large building. Carlos, aware of Mr. Musso's uncomfortable posture, said with a calm gesture, "Relax, Mr. Musso, and allow me to give you a tour."

Carlos escorted Nicholas and his entourage to another section of the warehouse, and they approached a large sliding door with several locks and chains. Carlos instructed one of his associates to unlock the doors and open them. The doors swung open to the view of a massive stack of clean, packaged drugs neatly laced approximately eight feet high and separated in four-foot increments with wooden pallets for transporting and placement. The width spanned over one hundred feet and a depth of at least fifty feet with thousands of packets orderly and in place. Nicholas, amazed at the enormity of it all, then responded, "Whoa!"

Carlos, vocalizing with excitement, stated, "Quite impressive, Mr. Nicholas, wouldn't you say?"

Nicholas came back with "Yes, I would say." Nicholas then questioned, "This is not all being moved on this trip?"

Carlos then explained, "Oh no, only a third of it on this trip is being shipped."

Nicholas with a very disturbed look exclaimed, "How do you plan to disguise this much stuff?"

Carlos explained, "Come—I will show you." They left the sealed-off area, and the doors swung closed and were locked behind them. Carlos, followed by Nicholas and the group, headed toward another area of the warehouse where an office with windows was sectioned off.

THE ASSAULT

From the Laredo Police Department, Rod called the Attorney General's office in Austin, Texas, and requested to speak with Mr. Tom Littleman, an assistant attorney under Ken Paxton, the AG. The secretary sent his call to Mr. Littleman's personal assistant, and she asked, "Who is calling?" and Rod replied, "This is Rod Tillman with the FBI, badge number 6205 with the Texas division, and I am calling about an urgent matter in reference to the Huntsville prison's recent breakout."

The assistant replied, "Yes, Mr. Tillman, let me see if I can reach him and have him call you back, if that is possible."

Rod returned with "That will be OK, but inform him of the urgency of my call."

She then assured him "I will, Officer Tillman" and documented Rod's phone number. Ten minutes passed, and Rod's cell rang, and the voice in an anxious tone explained, "Hello, Mr. Tillman—this is Tom Littleman with the Attorney General's office. How can I help you?"

Rod, with his matter-of-fact demeanor, responded, "Mr. Littleman, thank you for returning my call." Rod continued, "I am in the middle of a murder investigation that is connected to the recent breakout at the Huntsville prison, and I need your help."

A Latin-looking individual dressed in fatigues, black military boots, and a stocking hat stood on the ridge in the trees one hundred yards from the warehouse compound. He was aiming a missile launcher directly at the office window behind which Nicholas and Carlos had just sat down. He snapped open the covers on the missile launcher and fired directly into the metal building's window. The blast exploded out the glass section of the metal walls. Everyone inside was obliterated as the fire engulfed the office area. The guards outside scattered for cover and began shooting automatic weapons in the direction of the perpetrator. The Latin that had fired the weapon headed up the hill to an awaiting truck and left the scene undetected. Inside the office were the remains of the dead participants, including Carlos. Nicholas, who had been forced against a wall where remnants of metal file cabinets covered him face down, kicked his leg and moved his hand, showing some life. Some of the remaining staff, having run for cover upon the impact of the explosion, now, recirculating, noticed Nicholas moving and dragged him from the obliterated office.

Gus Lucas was sitting at a desk in his downtown Laredo warehouse office as one of his men, dressed in a slick black suit and white tie, approached him and leaned over his left shoulder and delivered a message to his ear. His eyes opened wide, and he turned abruptly and with a surprised expression said "What?" and followed with "They blew up the building?"

The man responded, "Yeah, boss, someone exploded the building and killed 'em all!"

Gus Lucas then stood up and shook his head and then frantically stated, "Let's get them on the line!"

His personal secretary rushed into the room and questioned, "What's going on?"

The black suit explained to her, "Ah, dem guys blew up the shop in Colombia and killed dem all!"

The secretary put her hand to her mouth and responded, "Oh my God, killed them all?"

In an obviously uneducated tone, he reiterated, "Yeah, they all dead!"

Lucas then interjected to the secretary, "See if you can get someone down there on the phone."

The secretary departed and went to another secretary, questioning who they could call to get a full account. Lucas left the room looking for one of his head guys, trying to come to some resolve and find out if the drugs were destroyed.

The news of the assault on Gus Lucas's drug warehouse in Colombia spread quickly. Rod got a call from Brad Kingsworth telling him of the bombing, and Rod sarcastically remarked, "Well, that probably ruined Gus Lucas's day, but hopefully it keeps them busy so I can get this stuff before a judge."

Brad then commented, "Rod, what are you going to do with that woman?"

Rod answered, "That is our only witness, and we need to protect her!"

Brad then upped his tone and demanded, "Rod, those guys have already attempted to take her out." He then mandated, "We got to get her testimony in front of a judge now!"

Rod replied, "Brad, I got her, and we are ready, but I need your help to get her into court!"

Brad ended with "All right, all right, let me see what I can do to expedite this case," and he finished with "I will get back to you. Keep her safe."

The front entrance to the Fresenius Medical Care hospital in Risaralda, Colombia, early in the morning was the scene. In the

THE RESOLVE

intensive care unit, viewing Nicholas lying on a surgical bed with bandaged head, hands, and arms, stood Gus Lucas. The nurse attendant in starched blue scrubs and a mask exited the glass enclosed unit, and Gus approached her to inquire as to his condition.

She first questioned, "Are you a family member, Señor?"

Gus responded, "Yes, I am his uncle."

The nurse then began her brief clinical but well-trained condition explanation. She stated, "He is still in critical condition but showing signs of improving, and we should be better informed once he responds to the medication."

Gus questioned, "When will I be able to talk to him?"

The nurse immediately retorted, "When the doctor releases him from ICU" as she now departed down the corridor.

Agent Troy McGinnis drove up to the Hyatt Regency in San Antonio and went to Katrina's room and knocked. Although Rod had called Katrina about changing hotels as a precautionary measure, she was still extremely apprehensive and asked, "Who's there?"

Troy responded, "It's me, Agent Troy McGinnis, second best to Rod Tillman." The offbeat humor relaxed her and at the same time reassured her it was Troy. She opened the door, and he said, "We need to move quickly. Are you ready?"

She then questioned, "Does anyone else know I am being relocated?"

Troy then explained, "No, just Rod and me, but I never know who is watching, and I don't want anyone becoming suspicious of your relocation."

THE ASSAULT

They quickly left the room and walked out of the hotel straight to Troy's vehicle, got in, and drove off. They headed to a nearby Hilton, where a room was registered under another agent's name. Upon entering the new room, Troy questioned Katrina, "Do you need anything?"

Katrina quickly asked, "I am hungry. How do I get something to eat here?"

Troy reiterated, "Use this agent's name or your room number to order anything you wish to eat, but always check the door before opening." Troy then said "Good-bye, and number one, Agent Tillman, will call you on this new phone" as he handed her the cell phone and left the room.

Agent Tim McCally, still stationed at the Huntsville prison, called Rod's cell, and Rod answered, "Yes, Agent McCally, what can I do for you today?"

McCally then asked, "I guess you are aware of Mr. Lucas's warehouse explosion down in Colombia?"

Rod responded, "Yes sir, I sure am, and this has brought to light a whole new arena of players connected with the Huntsville Unit breakout."

McCally then remarked, "I know you have a boatload of info on the subject—care to meet and share so we can begin resolving our issues here?"

Rod then, with an air of frustration, replied, "I hear what you are asking, Agent McCally, but we are at a strategic point where releasing too much at this time could cause us to backpedal."

McCally now, misunderstanding Rod's choice of words, raised his voice somewhat and cynically stated, "Mr. Tillman, I thought we were all on the same team and the sharing of information would benefit us all." McCally ended with "I guess I will have to go up the ladder to get what I need!"

Rod smirked and finished the conversation with an effort to soothe the wound with "Agent McCally, that is not my intention, but you may or may not know we have a key witness who has already had a life-threating assault, and we are not sure how the information got out, but we are now being very cautious."

Agent McCally quickly blurted out, "OK, Agent Tillman!" and hung up.

Rod picked up on the frustration of McCally and pondered how to put this tiger back in his cage. He then decided to call Brad, who answered with "Yes, Rod?"

Rod immediately pleaded, "Brad, McCally thinks I am avoiding him and doesn't understand my discretion in maintaining case silence for the moment as I am trying to keep Katrina safe."

Brad took a deep breath and replied, "I hear you, Rod. Let me give him a call and reassure him and see if I can't restore his confidence."

Rod, with a sigh of relief, responded, "Thank you, boss!"

CHAPTER 13
THE MONTENEGRO

Gus Lucas, now assessing the damaged site, looked at three of his workers standing in an attire of blue jeans, white denim shirts, and soft hats directly in front of him. Lucas then questioned them, "You have any idea who might have done this?"

Two of them responded at the same moment almost in sequence: "No, Señor Lucas, we never saw him!"

Lucas then proceeded toward the warehouse of stored drugs as one of the workers opened the sliding door. He breathed a sigh of relief as he observed all the many stacks neatly still in place. He paused with his hands on his hips and told the head worker "I want five, *cinco*, guards with guns, one at each door" as he pointed to the various doors. He then finished with "I want twenty-four-hour guards, and at no time, not even to take a piss, will you leave without a replacement, you *comprende?*" The worker shook his head in agreement and began gathering up the whole workforce as they scattered to get their weapons.

Rod called Katrina on the provided cell phone. She picked up and questioned, "Yes, who is this?"

THE RESOLVE

Rod replied in a sarcastic but firm tone, "It is me, and I am the only one who will call you on this phone!" He then added, "Remember that—it is important!"

She then sheepishly answered, "Yes, Mr. FBI Man—I mean, Rod—I understand." She then said in an excited voice, "When are you coming to see me?"

Rod now realized he might have created a monster and wondered how he was going to put the brakes on this now developing sordid affair. He replied with somewhat of a reassuring tone so as not to discourage her, "I will be there soon—if not tonight, by tomorrow at noon."

She said with a simpering expression, "Aw, please come tonight. I will have a surprise for you," and then passionately stated, "I miss you, Rod!"

Rod, not knowing how he should respond sympathetically, ended with "Katrina, I do want to see you, but your protection is my first concern, and I need to resolve a number of issues before I come over there" and then completed the call with "I will call you before I come" and hung up before she could reply. Rod looked around the room to see if anyone overheard his conversation and then, with his usual lip curl, walked off.

—⚭—

Large covered trucks, one after the other, were rolling into the port on the coast of Colombia near the Venezuelan border as Gus Lucas stood with a Panamanian white-brimmed hat, watching from a distance. He turned and faced Nicholas, who was in a wheelchair, with bandages across his face and down his arms. Gus, in an expression of sympathy, asked Nicholas, "How are you feeling, my friend?"

Nicholas, through the bandaged, wrapped face, replied "I will be ready."

Gus then exclaimed, "We will get those hombres that did this to you."

Nicholas then, in an exasperated tone, answered, "Look, Gus, I just want to get the fuck out of here."

In that moment, Victoria, dressed in a white, tight-fitting, full-length dress, with a black belt around her waist accentuating her tall and slender figure, walked up behind Nicholas seated in the wheelchair. Nicholas turned slightly and observed her presence along with her beauty. Gus immediately explained with an introduction, "You met my daughter, Victoria?"

Nicholas responded with somewhat of a questioning, slow answer: "Yes, and she is here because?"

Gus then laid out the plan for Nicholas: "You and Victoria will be traveling as a couple, and as it has come to be, we will use this unfortunate tragedy to our advantage."

Nicholas questioned with now a tone of uncertainty, "Tragedy?"

Gus looked Nicholas straight in the eye and continued, "Since you are in this condition, you will be traveling to receive medical assistance in the United States."

Nicholas suspiciously said, "You sure this wasn't the plan from the start?"

Gus immediately answered, "You think I would take a chance on killing you after all the trouble I went to to get you here?"

Nicholas now turned around, staring at Victoria up and down, and again responded to Gus in a low tone: "Nothing would surprise me about what you do, Gus."

THE RESOLVE

Rod knocked on the hotel door to Katrina's room, but no one answered. Rod knocked again, and still no response. He began to think the worst and flashed his badge to a cleaning attendant, who in turn went to a house phone and calls the desk. Within three minutes, a tall black gentlemen in a suit with a brass shiny name tag and hotel insignia stepped off the elevator and greeted Rod. Rod, in a panic mode, again flashed his credentials to the gentleman, who instructed the attendant to open the door. Rod rushed past the tall man to first see if she had been murdered but observed that she was nowhere to be found. More importantly, Rod observed that all her luggage was gone. He contemplated for a moment and concluded that if she were abducted they would not have taken time to remove her luggage and all her belongings. He questioned the manager and requested him to allow him access to their surveillance cameras at all ground-floor exits. The cameras showed her leaving at about 8:15 a.m. with her luggage and accessories in a hotel loading cart. She got into a cab and was driven off.

Rod, after having observed the identity of the cab, jumped into his vehicle and headed straight to the company building. He went straight to the dispatcher's cage and again pulled out his badge and provided a quick but somewhat minimal reason he needed to know the route of that particular cab this morning. He then learned she went to the bus station. He again took off for the bus station, hoping to catch her before she got on a bus. He next dashed into the main terminal and began searching, and as luck would have it, he spotted her sitting in a remote corner with her head turned to the wall. Obviously, she was attempting to be obscured from everyone around. Rod walked up and put his hand on her shoulder, and she jumped in fear. He softly questioned, "You forget about our lunch date?"

Now, with a look of apology, she replied, "You did not come last night, and I am very worried about my family and was going to Mexico City to check on them."

Rod then picked up her suitcase and stated calmly, "Your family is fine. They are being watched by my people." He then, feeling so relieved he caught her before she left, added, "Let's go get some lunch."

Victoria now pushed Nicholas in the wheelchair along the gangway, boarding the cargo ship *Montenegro*. The numerous containers were now being loaded in the cargo area of the ship. The steel ramp lead to an area below the bridge that was well decorated with high-gloss wood flooring, wall prints and somewhat of a formal atmosphere, especially for a cargo ship. Victoria continued to wheel Nicholas, following a steward to a cabin door, which he opened, and they entered. Their luggage was already in place. A large port window lightened the room with a view of the opposite shoreline of the commercial port. Hillside white housing with terra-cotta-lined roofs cascaded over the heavily green forested terrain. Victoria handed the steward a roll of cash as if to say, "Be vigilant of our needs." The steward nodded in acceptance of the task and closed the door as he departed. Nicholas stood up from the chair and began removing the bandages from his face and then turned to look at Victoria, displaying only minor, small burn scars on his forehead, and questioned, "Now what?"

Rod was now having a conversation on a cell phone from Katrina's room with Brad Kingsworth. He was demanding to Brad, "When can we get a judge in front of this?" He continued in a low tone as Katrina went into the bathroom, "I don't think she is going to stand around here forever, Brad."

Brad replied, "I hear you. Let me see if I can get her with the Attorney General and move this case to the forefront!" He finished with "Do you think we have enough now to make some arrests?"

Rod came back quickly, "It depends on how much she is willing to divulge, and that depends on how safe she feels."

Brad ended with "Will she accept some form of witness protection?"

Rod, with a defeatist innuendo, said, "Well, she left us just to go check on her family without a care of who may have been watching her." Rod then tightened his lips and closed with "I just don't know what she will do, Brad. I just don't know."

The *Montenegro* sailed into the port harbor in Haiti, and Nicholas stared out the window at the scenery. Victoria was coming out of the shower in a white robe. She inquired, "Are we pulling into port?"

Nicholas turned toward her and admired the beauty of her long brown hair streaming over her shoulders and the penetration of her green eyes staring straight at him. Her sleekness was silhouetted by the background of the bathroom light. He responded, "Yes, it appears we are about to dock."

Victoria informed him, as she gave off the sense of approval of his rugged physique and the mystique of his former prison life, "My father has plans to offload our cargo and provide a disguise for shipping and then reload." She continued with "We will be here for two days." Nicholas thought the process was apparent as he sat down on the desk chair sideways, folded his arms, and looked intently as Victoria slipped a dress shirt over her head and pulled white pants up to her navel. The obvious attraction between the two was looming in the dimly lit room. Victoria broke the ice and spurted out, "Yes, you know I want you, but now is not the moment; we have work to do." Nicholas, with a smirk on his face, nodded in agreement.

Gus Lucas was now back in Laredo and calling Victoria on his cell phone. She finally answered after several rings. His frustrated tone was expressed when he questioned, "Where are you? You should have been there!"

She answered, "We just arrived at the port, and it looks like the containers are being unloaded."

Gus inquired, "How is Nicholas?"

She responded, "Appears to be doing much better."

Gus, in his paternal nature, asked, "He didn't try anything with you in the same cabin?"

She, in a casual manner and tone, said, "No, he's not that well and has been the perfect gentleman."

Gus then resolved, "He knows who he is dealing with and will respect that!"

Victoria then concluded in an effort to end this conversation, "We need to get down to the dock."

Gus turned his attention to the caution of the unloading and the proposed concealment operations and impressed upon her, "Go and make sure they do it right!"

Victoria shut off the phone and turned to Nicholas, who now had an expression showing that he understood Gus and his fatherly concerns and stated, "As you say, we have work to do. We need to go." Victoria, with an even more intense look of lust, smiled at Nicholas as they went out the cabin door.

Rod, sitting on the edge of the hotel room bed with Katrina next to him, explained, "I have lined up the attorney general, and he will take a statement from you tomorrow at 2:00 p.m."

Katrina, with a worried look on her face, questioned, "Will you be with me?" and Rod answered, "All the way."

He then interjected, "Katrina, you will be safe, and no one will be aware of your testimony until they have been arrested and we are in court."

Katrina, with total fear in her eyes, then asked, "Suppose they are not convicted or let free on bond—then they can get to me or my family!"

Rod reassured her, "I promise that will never happen!" He then reaffirmed with "Gus Lucas's arrest will be so airtight when we get him in the courtroom he will be headed straight to lockup."

Katrina, realizing the far-reaching possibilities that existed with Gus Lucas and his ruthless cartel operations, and exhibiting a much-concerned tone, again questioned Rod, "What if he even from prison decides to get back at me and my family?"

Rod, understanding the realization of her thoughts, impressed upon her the eminent need for her to consider the witness protection program as he explained, "Katrina, you need to take advantage of the witness protection. Please think about it!"

Katrina then pleaded, "Rod, what about my family? He can get to them, and I can't live with that no matter how much you protect me!"

Rod, truly comprehending her dilemma, asked, "How many family members, and who are they?"

She then in an exasperated demeanor shouted, "Rod, my mother, my sister, my two brothers, and their children. There are many!"

The overwhelming depth of Katrina's factual truths about the long reach of Gus Lucas and his cartel connections was now becoming very worrisome to Rod as he sat for a moment in contemplation of her intense, realistic fear for her family. He again turned to her with a very direct, penetrating look and agreed with her and stated, "OK, I understand your concerns, and I will consult with Brad about relocating, at the FBI's expense, your whole family."

Katrina in response explained, "They will never leave and do not understand my situation."

Rod, finally in full comprehension, ended with "We will provide round-the-clock protection until Lucas is put away!"

CHAPTER 14
PORT OF MOBILE

Nicholas and Victoria were standing in a warehouse as each of the containers was unloaded next to a large steel tank. The steel tank, which was filled with a mixture of diluted sugar and water for the proposed concealment of the transported product, was in place in the warehouse. The carefully wrapped packages stacked on wood pallets were removed with a forklift and placed in the storage area of the warehouse. Fiberglass containers were then placed in the warehouse with an open end. The pallets of products were forklifted and placed in the fiberglass containers with open-ended walls and then sealed in position. Each container was then filled via a flexible hose extending from the tank filled with sugar water, which was pumped to a pipe stem mounted above each fiberglass container. Each container was filled with the mixture to a set level. The containers, now very heavy, were reloaded on the trucks and returned to the ship for placement back on the ship. Nicholas and Victoria left the site in a black limo and looked at each other with a satisfied feeling that this was moving along well so far. Once at the ship dock, they headed up the gangplank and met the steward on deck, who escorted them back to the cabin.

PORT OF MOBILE

The steward opened the cabin door, and both Nicholas and Victoria entered, and Nicholas pulled the handle behind him as Victoria turned and stared at him in moment of total silence. Then, in a passionate rage, they embraced and began undressing, pulling their clothes off while kissing continually and falling onto the bed. Nicholas paused in the moment and in a low tone questioned, "Maybe we are taking a risk that was not in your father's plan?"

Victoria, with a bit of disappointment obvious, responded, "Do not ever think you know what my father is planning." She then rolled over on top of Nicholas, pushed his arms against the bed headboard, and continued with "He considers everyone as being expendable, so relax, because he doesn't give a damn about you!" She then concluded with "We are all part of the plan." Nicholas, realizing she was right, stared into her eyes and then pulled her to him, forcing himself back on top of her.

—~—

Troy McGinnis was standing at the front desk of the Laredo Police Department as two gentlemen in gray suits with black ties walked in and identified themselves as US marshals here on the investigation of the Huntsville prison breakout, and the lead, the taller of the two, stated, "I understand you have in custody two suspects who attempted to take out your lead witness." He then asked, "We would like to question the two witnesses; are they here?"

The desk sergeant, scoping them out, turned to Troy, who was listening to the two interested marshals and finally turned to them and introduced himself. "I am FBI agent Troy McGinnis, one of the chief investigators on this case." He then inquired, "Why are the US marshals taking an interest in this case?"

The same tall gentleman responded, "We are investigating on behalf of the Attorney General, and it has been brought to our attention that you were interrogating two possible connections."

Troy, now believing that there was some validity to their claims, told the sergeant, "I will take them back, Sergeant. Let the holding cell personnel know I am coming back." The sergeant responded but noticed their holstered weapons and demanded, "OK, Mr. FBI, but those two have to leave their weapons here with me until they walk out." The marshals, expecting the routine, unshouldered their guns and handed them to the desk sergeant as they followed Troy through the door leading to the back.

Then returning from assuring Katrina's safety in San Antonio, Rod pulled up to the Laredo police station. Troy was escorting the two US marshals down the hall and told the police attendant who he was and that they needed to see the two suspects in custody. The attendant buzzed the door lock, and the door slid open, and they headed to the cell where the two, still in their suits, were sitting. Troy, somewhat puzzled by their information, was thinking, How would they know that we have these two locked up? And then, as the cell door began to slide open, the two henchmen looked up and obviously recognized the two marshals, and their expressions, with half smiles yet a bit of suspicion across their faces, alerted Troy that something wasn't quite right. In the moment the shorter of the marshals pulled out a weapon from his back and shot Troy square in the chest, and he fell to the floor. The taller of the two also pulled out a hidden gun and exclaimed to the two in the cell, "Gus says hello and goodbye!" as he shot both of them each in the temple. The two disguised perpetrators now headed to the cellblock door and pointed a gun at the uniformed attendant and exclaimed, "It's

PORT OF MOBILE

not worth dying over!" The block door opened, and the short one still shot the attendant, who fell over the desk as they jetted up the hallway toward the front exit.

Rod, now at the entrance, heard all the gunfire, pulled his weapon, and yelled to the desk sergeant to hide as the tall perpetrator exited into the entrance first. He saw Rod and fired, but Rod ducked behind a concrete support post as the bullet ricocheted, chipping a concrete fragment. The taller individual made it out the front door with continual firing of his weapon. The shorter perpetrator arrived to the entrance from the rear, not seeing Rod, who placed two rounds in his head, and he fell to the floor. Rod immediately ran out the entrance as the escaped individual was driving off. Rod placed numerous rounds into the rear of the vehicle, but to no avail. Rod then returned to the entrance, looked over the counter, and saw the sergeant hidden behind the desk, but not injured. He then rushed to the back and observed the uniformed attendant face down on the desk. He checked for a pulse but realized he was dead. He then, with the cellblock door still opened, headed to the back and saw Troy sitting up against a portal wall, staring at the two dead henchmen. Rod immediately questioned, after noticing no blood on the chest that Troy was holding with his hand in pain, "Are you shot?" Troy answered with a gasp of breath, "I was!" Troy then pulled open his shirt and exposed the bulletproof vest.

Rod then looked at Troy, who now sat with an open shirt and had a totally flustered look on his face, and said, "What is it with you? Every time I ask you to keep an eye on witnesses, they get shot and die!"

Troy responded, still breathing heavily, "Yes, well, this time they shot me!"

Rod took a deep breath and shook his head in agreement as he murmured, "Yes, they did, and that concerns me." He continued, "It is obvious they will stop at nothing, even killing FBI agents, to get what they want!" He then, in a low tone, thinking out loud, expressed, "We have to step it up, Troy, because they won't even think twice about eliminating Katrina." He then, as he looked off into the room, explained to Troy, "There is something big that was or is still coming from that warehouse in Colombia, and we need to find that out and where it is going!" He then followed with "Brad Kingsworth is going to have to approve a vacation trip for you and me to visit South America." He then looked at Troy and questioned, "That is, if you are up to it?" Troy answered immediately, as he began to stand up, "Oh, I am good to go!"

The *Montenegro* was now entering the port harbor in Mobile, with Victoria standing on the steel ship deck, her silhouette being shadowed against the metal wall by the sun as she stared at the large crane structures unloading cargo containers in the distance. Nicholas, who was gazing at her beauty from the cabin door, informed her in a loud tone, to get her attention above the ship noise, "We will be docking very soon!" He then added, "Do you want to change? Because we head out from here."

Victoria shook her head in agreement and walked back to the cabin. She explained to Nicholas, "The containers will be directly loaded onto barges and shipped west."

Nicholas, with a look of surprise, questioned, "West?" and then again questioned, "where are they headed?"

Victoria, realizing her father had given only her all the details but needed Nicholas for his male tenacity and willingness to do most anything for the right money, gave him only limited information. She then answered, "Everything will be clear soon."

Nicholas, now somewhat insulted, sarcastically asked, "I thought I was taken out of prison to lead this operation and you were assisting me?"

Victoria, now sensing his ego had been bruised, attempted to placate the situation with "You are, Nicholas, but he is keeping us both safe as we reach each stage of this operation by making sure we individually don't know the whole plan, and this minimizes any slip of the tongue in our conversation."

Nicholas rolled his eyes and responded, "Don't play me for a fool, Victoria. Where are we headed?" She then, in a low voice, answered, "I will tell you when I know no one can hear us." She then looked up and pointed to the light fixture in the cabin as if to indicate a possible hidden microphone. Nicholas, partially satisfied with that explanation, decided to leave it until later.

Gus Lucas was getting into a black Lincoln with a driver. The large steel door automatically rolled up, and there stood Rod in the entrance, holding his badge up at eye level. His left hand was on his badge and his right was on his holstered revolver. Gus and the driver looked surprised as Rod yelled out, "Gus Lucas, you are under arrest!" One of Gus's henchmen, who had been hiding behind the left side of the roll-up door, walked out with a shotgun in hand. Rod without hesitation put a shot into his leg, and he fell to the ground. Rod exclaimed, "What part of this badge do you not understand?" In that moment, Gus opened his door and stepped out as the driver remained silently in place. Rod turned toward the vehicle and cuffed him and patted him down for a weapon while he informed him he was a suspect in the murder of a police officer and two witnesses in incarceration. He then Mirandized him and walked him to his vehicle.

Gus questioned, "What proof do you have I have any involvement in these murders?"

Rod, in a perfect lie, responded, "Well, we wounded one of your assassins, and he's singing your name!"

Gus then, with a worried look, answered, "Anyone can make such a statement because of my being well known in the community."

Rod, with a roll of the eyes, came back with "Yes, you are well known in the community, all right, and that is why we have no hesitation about bringing you in for questioning."

Nicholas and Victoria departed the ship via a metal gangway ramp and headed straight to a customs departure gate. After passing through customs, they headed to the longshoremen's parking lot, where a late-model metallic gray Buick was parked. Victoria, already informed about the vehicle and its location, whipped out a set of keys while they were continuing toward the vehicle. Nicholas, with an inquisitive facial expression, expressed in a low, sarcastic tone, "I guess this is just more information I am not aware of." He then continued with his sarcasm as his vocal tone began to rise. "Anyone can see I am in charge of this operation."

Victoria sensed his obvious frustration and replied to his comments with "Give it a break, Nicholas. These are just the small details he sent me along to assist you with." She then added, "Do you think I have no brains and could not possibly possess some knowledge of a detail here and there to back you up with in this very involved operation?"

Nicholas then calmed down and shook his head in agreement and softened his reply with "Yeah, you're right, I see your point." They then got in the vehicle, and Victoria, behind the wheel, turned to Nicholas and informed him, "By the way, we are headed to New Orleans." They then pulled out of the parking lot.

Rod pulled his car into the back of the Laredo police station and opened the back door as Gus Lucas stepped out onto the pavement. Rod escorted him to the rear electronic door and flashed his badge to the camera being watched by an officer internally, who then pushed a button releasing the door lock. Rod then walked him to the front arresting desk sergeant for processing before placing him into a cell. Gus then, in a frustrated tone, questioned, "Is this going to take very long?" He then stated, "I have a business to run and cannot be detained all day, especially if you only have hearsay."

Rod then turned and faced him and reacted with a cool tone. "Mr. Lucas, you are not going to be conducting any outside business for the rest of this day, but this station has a very nice meal and great accommodations for you!" Rod then finished with "Do you think if I only had hearsay, I would have picked you up?" Rod then raised his eyebrows as if to ask "Is there something else?" and then turned and walked away, leaving Gus with the sergeant.

Upon feeling secure with Lucas in the cuffs with the sergeant, Rod called Brad on his cell phone and informed him, "I have Gus Lucas in custody."

Brad questioned, "What did you charge him with?"

Rod immediately answered, "Murder."

Brad turned his head with a sense of doubt and responded, "Murder of whom?" He became even more inquisitive and continued on, "Rod, he wasn't at the station!"

Rod, in his wit, stated, "I know. I lied to him and told him the remaining dead goon, left behind, ratted on him to save his neck!" Rod concluded with "He didn't believe me, as he knew his henchman feared him more than the police." Rod then requested that Brad come to Laredo and help him interrogate Lucas.

CHAPTER 15
CANECO SUGAR

Victoria and Nicholas pulled up to the Hilton hotel along the Mississippi River in New Orleans at the end of Poydras Street. Nicholas stared at the uniformed valet opening Victoria's door as she handed a twenty-dollar bill to the young man with the keys. She instructed the valet as she moved from the open vehicle door, "Keep it available—we may need it in the morning."

The valet responded "Yes ma'am" and stepped into the vehicle, started the engine, and drove away. Victoria, next whipping out a credit card at the front desk, turned and looked back at Nicholas with a coy look and asked, "One room or two?"

Nicholas in an impulse responded, "Why waste your father's money?" Nicholas then followed Victoria into the elevator, and she grabbed his belt buckle and pulled him to her bosom and bit him on his chin. The arousal intrigued Nicholas as he pushed her to the back wall in the elevator. The door opened on the eighth floor, and two children stepped in and focused on them. Nicholas turned and with a cynical expression murmured to the children, "Does either of you have a camera?" No movement or vocal responses from the children as the elevator now reached the fourteenth floor, and both Nicholas and Victoria exited. Victoria reached the room door first and keyed the lock, and as it opened, she then turned to Nicholas, made a quirky lip movement, and proceeded through the door. The two then fell on the bed into a passionate embrace and again began pulling off their clothes.

Brad Kingsworth now, after having arrived in Laredo, stared across the table at Gus Lucas in the police department investigation room. Brad took a deep breath and slowly released his air as he looked at his notes. He then looked up at Gus and sarcastically asked, "Mr. Lucas, do you think we are totally unaware of all your illicit activities and attacks and the extraction of Mr. Nicholas Musso from our inescapable Huntsville detention facility?"

Gus sat back in the chair and folded his arms and in a very slow demeanor answered Brad, "Well, there you go, Mr. FBI Man, trying to solve all your problems by blaming the immigrants because you just want to put us in jail!"

Brad chuckled to himself and then responded, "Mr. Lucas, is that going to be your defense—because you think that our bumbling detective work all comes down to incarcerating notorious underworld characters such as yourself as our reaction to immigration?" Brad continued, "Our evidence and your defense are going to make the judge's decision an easy one!" He then finished with "Mr. Lucas, do you want to help yourself, or should we just move forward with all our witnesses and investigation straight to court?"

Gus looked up from the floor and questioned, "What witnesses?"

CANECO SUGAR

Rod called Katrina on her new phone as she sat in the room watching TV, eating snacks she ordered from the hotel's in-room menu. She answered with an anxious tone in her voice, "Who is this?" and Rod stated, "It's me."

She quickly retorted, "Aren't you supposed to be more explaining than that?"

Rod then answered, "Yes, well, maybe we should set up some kind of a code."

Katrina then questioned, "Code?" and Rod explained, "Yeah, like I say 'apple' and you say 'orange' and that way we know it is us."

Katrina then asked, "When am I going to see you again?" and Rod responded, "I will be there in the morning." He then added, "I arrested Gus Lucas, and he is in the Laredo Police Department jail."

Katrina then, with a very worried expression, replied, "His men will be coming to get me."

Rod then reassured her, "No, no, he is worried about his own neck right now and not thinking about you. He has no idea of your whereabouts." Rod then finished with "Calm down. Gus thinks we have one of his henchmen in custody spilling the beans."

Katrina relaxed and ended with "Please come early." Rod then turned off his cell.

—⚞—

Victoria and Nicholas, twenty-four hours later, were back in the vehicle, headed southeast from New Orleans along Louisiana Highway 39 to Chalmette. The destination was the Caneco Sugar refinery along the Mississippi River. Upon arriving at the docks at the refinery, Victoria pulled the vehicle up to the edge of the wooden ramp and sat and gazed at the ships moving up and down the river. She then turned toward Nicholas and said, "How long do you think it will be before they get here?"

Nicholas responded, "Well, didn't they say it would take twenty-four hours for them to get here?" Sixty minutes passed, and Nicholas noticed the spotlight of the tugboat pushing the barges with the containers approaching. The barges were aligned with the receiving platform, and the tugboat captain positioned the barges to be moored alongside the dock. Dock workers were throwing ropes on the cleats and shoring up the first barge. Victoria and Nicholas stepped out of the vehicle and walked toward the lighted portside shipment security station.

Piping was set in place to pump the sugar-water solution from each of the containers. Just as connections were being completed to the outlets of the containers, an employee of the sugar company approached and questioned, "Is each of the containers full of liquid sugar solution?"

One of the boat crew turned and replied in half English and half Spanish, "*Si*, Señor, full of juice." The employee then instructed the boat crewman to begin pulling the flexible hose for connection to the dock container tank.

The foreman, a tall, heavyset man, then approached the Caneco dock employee questioning the shipment, and the employee then explained, "Yes, Chief, we received papers last week."

The chief, not recognizing this individual, demanded, "Who are you? And show me the manifest."

Then, within an instant, the chief was hit from behind with a blunt weapon and knocked unconscious to the ground. After the man fell, Nicholas stood in the light with a club in hand. Nicholas then stated "Gag him and tie him up and put him in that shop over there" as he pointed to the dock house.

The tugboat captain, then concerned, questioned, "But he has seen our faces!"

Nicholas immediately answered, "You can take the $10,000 and scatter after you unload these tanks, and he will never know where you have gone, so get movin'!"

The tank solutions were pumped into an adjacent receiving tank that was recently set in place. Five flatbed trucks and trailers pulled up to receive the drained containers. One of the trailers had an attached forklift, which was unloaded as the containers were being removed by the refinery's crane per the paid-off operator. The continued manipulation and direct attention to the unloading and reloading process by the foreign workers was not realized by Caneco's employees in all the confusion. That is, until two regular employees came looking for the chief. Nicholas, now becoming very concerned, opened the car door and grabbed his 9-millimeter and clip from the glove compartment. Victoria rushed up to him and pushed him backward against the vehicle and quietly mumbled, "Hold it—no shooting here tonight!" She then added, "Too many trucks, too much very expensive merchandise, and we would never get out of here!" She then finished, "Stay put and let me handle this."

Victoria next headed straight toward the two questioning employees and with some assertion said, "Excuse me—are you with Caneco?"

One of the employees responded, "Yes, I am the shop steward, and who are you?"

Victoria immediately answered, "We are with the Florida Sugar Co-op and came to deliver the liquid sugar solution shipment from

Mobile that was to be unloaded for processing by Caneco." Victoria now, with some ease and confidence, edged further into the deceit with "The other gentleman said he didn't have the manifest and left to go check in your main offices."

The same employee then, with somewhat of an embarrassed tone, stuttered and stated, "That was Mr. Winston, our night chief." Victoria was waiting for further explanation from the employee when the employee exclaimed, "Well, OK, I guess he will be back." The two employees then departed.

The trucks were finally loaded and began pulling out, headed for Louisiana Highway 39, while the tugboat pulled away from the dock. Nicholas and Victoria immediately got back in their vehicle and followed the trucks. Nicholas turned to Victoria and in a sheepish tone interjected, "I guess that was the reason your father sent you along!"

Victoria then responded, with a voice of control but not overwhelming, "Yes, Nick, we all have our expertise and place in this world."

Rod drove up to the Hilton in San Antonio and parked. He looked up at the hotel and meditated for a moment, took a deep breath, and opened his car door. Rod looked around the front desk area as he entered the hotel to see if anyone suspicious was following him. He then pushed the elevator button, and the door opened, and there stood Katrina, crying in fear, and an armed assailant directly behind her with a gun in her back. Rod immediately reacted and pulled his weapon and gripped it with both hands, aiming at the temple of the assailant. The perpetrator demanded, "Either put down the weapon and step away, or I am going to drop her right here!"

Rod, in a calm, cool demeanor, responded, "Then what, I shoot you in the head?" He then continued, "How about we all walk to your vehicle outside and you leave without anyone shooting anyone?"

The perpetrator, in a sarcastic tone, answered, "Oh yeah, you are just going to let me drive away?"

Rod fired his weapon in an instant and struck the assailant in the center of the forehead. The individual stood immobile with a look of surprise and then dropped to the floor.

Katrina, in relief, fell toward Rod, and he embraced her in his arms. She exclaimed to Rod, "I can't take this anymore!"

Rod, at a loss for words and realizing her predicament, expressed in a low tone, "So breakfast is out?"

Katrina looked up at him and complained, "Do you have any sense of what I am going through?"

Rod, now in a compassionate voice, insisted, "Let's get you out of here!"

The sirens and San Antonio police were now swarming the area, moving interested onlookers back away from the scene. Rod flashed his credentials and badge to the lead sergeant in charge and escorted Katrina out the front door. The sergeant exclaimed, "We need her for questioning, so don't go too far."

Rod replied, "I will bring her in."

The sergeant added, "We need you too!"

Rod ended with "I know, sergeant. We are not leaving town."

The five flatbeds of cargo had pulled off I-10 just east of Lake Charles, Louisiana, into a large truck stop, alongside many other trucks parked for the night. The drivers were instructed to spread

THE RESOLVE

out and mix in with other transports and cover the cargo with tarps specifically selected for each truck to disguise the identity of the cargo. The next morning the trucks and trailers were pulling out separately at thirty-minute intervals of each other to avoid the suspected convoy appearance. They were all headed west to Laredo. Nicholas and Victoria, having spent the night at a nearby motel, were now sitting in the truck stop café sipping coffee, waiting for the last truck to exit the lot. Nicholas, staring at the clock on the wall and noticing the time was twenty-one past seven, turned to Victoria, who had focused her beautiful brown eyes directly on him above her positioned coffee mug. Nicholas informed Victoria, "You know, if they haven't already, it's just a matter of time before they find that refinery boss tied up in that dock house."

Victoria, in her usual confident demeanor, sipped her coffee and provided Nicholas with her own personal resolve. "They are looking for a convoy of five trucks with no coverage, and if the cargo were illegal, they would not have stopped overnight at a truck stop to rest."

Nicholas sat back in his chair, puckered his lips, and eased out with a satisfied expression, "You are probably right." They both continued to watch the truck-and-trailer rigs pull out of the parking lot at the set thirty-minute time spacings. It was now 7:30 a.m., and the fourth diesel engine cranked up as the smoke puffed from the vertical exhaust pipe. Nicholas turned to Victoria and stated the obvious: "Four down and one to go." In the distance, a faint sound of sirens could be heard headed their way. They both got up and exited the front door and then got into their vehicle. They drove out and onto the I-10 West onramp.

Victoria and Nicholas were now driving west toward Laredo when Nicholas questioned Victoria, "Will we make it to Laredo today?"

Victoria sarcastically responded, "I hope so, because the stress is wearing on me."

Nicholas then answered, "Actually, I have enjoyed being with you!"

Victoria again added, "You are a sexy son of a bitch, Nick, but we both know this is a temporary relationship, so I am not giving up my heart here!"

Nicholas, feeling somewhat insulted and with a loss of sensitivity at this point, importuned to Victoria, "So you feel nothing, and a heart surgeon would be wasting his time, as you have no heart!"

Victoria turned and looked hard at Nicholas and exclaimed, "Really?"

CHAPTER 16
THE BETRAYAL

Rod and Katrina were driving down I-35 South to Laredo and had basically ignored the local police request to come to the station. Rod was on his cell, in an anxious voice explaining to Brad Kingsworth the situation. "Brad, they got to her again! Lucas's man had a gun on her and was marching her out of the building, and if I had not been there…"

Brad immediately cut him short. "Slow down, Rod. Is she with you?"

Rod then looked over at her, and she sat with her head down, shaking with fear. He responded in a low tone, "Yes sir, she is in the vehicle, and we are headed back to Laredo."

Brad then reassured him, "I am here in Laredo, so get her back here to the station. Hell, they are all over San Antonio looking for her."

Rod then interjected, "You need to call the San Antonio local precinct near the Hilton and explain to that arresting sergeant that she is under witness protection and won't be coming in for a statement."

Brad replied, "Yes, let me get on the phone with him, and I want the ID of that shooter."

Gus Lucas was now sitting across the table in the interrogation room, with his overweight attorney poised to address Brad as he was about to enter. The moment he walked in, the attorney began his spiel: "Mr. Kingsworth, if all you have is suspicion and conjecture to hold my client and no actual documented facts, then I am demanding his immediate release!"

Brad looked down at the table, tapping his thumbs on the surface edge, then looked up at both Lucas and the attorney and abruptly stated, "You are free to go, but not too far, as we are about to bring those suspicions and conjecture to reality." Gus Lucas exchanged a hard stare with Brad as he and the attorney rose form their seats and exited through the door.

Nicholas and Victoria had now passed the Texas-Louisiana state line traveling on I-10 West and were trying to catch up to the first truck, which had a two-and-a-half-hour head start. The truck drivers were instructed not to exceed seventy miles per hour and to minimize their stops. They were also warned to stay off the cell phones unless they received a call from one number, Victoria's cell. Victoria was showing some concern in her face, as they should now be near the third truck. She called on her cell phone and got no response. They both looked at each other and then noticed a cloud of smoke billowing up as they approached a truck stop at an exit just east of Beaumont. They pulled off I-10, and as they were driving up to the parking area of the truck stop, they observed one of their units on fire in the middle of the lot, segregated from all the other tractor-trailer rigs parked on the site. The trailer of cargo was not in sight. Nicholas looked at

THE RESOLVE

Victoria, and in a panicked tone, she exclaimed, "My God, what is going on?"

Nicholas, now intently facing Victoria with frustration in his expression, responded, "We have been sabotaged and robbed." He continued, "Someone knew our plan and stole our gold."

They both noticed the driver standing away from the truck as they pulled up to him, and Victoria jumped out of the barely stopped vehicle and ran over to the driver, screaming, "What the hell is going on?"

The driver, with a torn shirt and dirty jeans, ran up to her crying, "Señorita, a man with a gun." He stammered, "He, he got out of the truck behind me and put a gun to my head and took my trailer." The driver ranted on, "He poured diesel in the window and made me unhook my trailer!" He finished with "I thought he was going to kill me, but he left with the trailer."

Victoria, with a look of surprise on her face, questioned the driver: "Did you see what he looked like?" She, now trying to understand and contemplate their next move, turned to Nicholas and in an emotional and excited voice said, "What's happening?" She turned back to the bewildered driver and questioned, "What color was his truck?"

The driver then looked down as if he was thinking and then, with a very ethnic Spanish dialogue, stated, "It was white, Señorita." He reassured her again, "It was white."

Nicholas immediately turned and got back into the vehicle and started the engine.

Victoria ran over and asked, "Where are you going?"

Nicholas answered, "You stay here, and I will see if I can catch him." He then pulled off in a swirl and left before she responded.

He looked in the rearview mirror at Victoria standing with her hands on her hips with a disgusted look on her face.

Rod and Katrina now walked into the Laredo police station and then entered where Brad was seated at a table in the same investigation room where he had interrogated Gus Lucas a few hours earlier. Rod walked in with Katrina behind him and asked, "You have Lucas in a holding cell?"

Brad answered, in an exasperated voice, "No, I had to let him go."

Rod immediately asked in a high vocal tone, "Why?"

Brad then responded, "Because he had his attorney and I had no factual evidence to hold him."

Rod then questioned, "Who is his attorney?"

Brad then, in the same exasperated voice, quipped back with "Paco, Taco Bell, hell, I don't know—just some local fandango lawyer who knows that you can't keep even a murderer like Gus Lucas without concrete evidence." Brad then noticed Katrina standing behind Rod with a look of fear in her eyes. Brad stood up and offered her a chair and with a sympathetic voice said, "I am so sorry, Ms. Katrina. Would you like to come in and sit?" Brad continued with "I promise you we will get Lucas and he will never bother you again."

Katrina looked up at Brad with a worried look on her face and, with a total expression of doubt, responded, "I don't feel very safe, Mr. Kingsworth."

Nicholas pulled off at the next exit and saw the white truck and trailer parked on the side of the road. Nicholas then drove alongside to the right and pushed the button to lower the passenger window. He then yelled at the truck driver, "Follow me." The truck then commenced to follow him down the two-lane road to a roadside motel. Nicholas then exited his vehicle and walked over to the driver's side of the cab and explained to the driver, "You pull in here and park for the night."

The driver then questioned, "What about the police?"

Nicholas quickly answered, "They are not going to call the police." Nicholas ended with "Park in the back, and I will meet you in the lobby."

Gus Lucas, now standing in the warehouse at Cortez Street and McClelland Avenue, was discussing on his cell phone with Victoria the stealing of one of his trucks. He questioned, "Where is Nicholas?"

Victoria, in frustration, explained, "He took off after them."

Gus questioned, "He left you there alone?"

She then tried to compensate with "Well, I guess with the fire, he figured someone would have to answer to the police and fire department."

Gus then replied, "Can't you call him on his cell phone?"

Victoria, now with a look of suspicion, complained, "I will keep trying, but I have to get out of here!"

Gus then stated, "Call me back in an hour and let me know, and I will be sending someone to pick you up." Gus finished with "Have you had any word on the other trucks?"

She then contemplated for a moment and stated, "One of them should be showing up in the next couple of hours, but if not, then we need to start backtracking." She then closed with "Get someone here quickly."

Rod, heading back to his hotel room with Katrina in the passenger seat staring out the window, explained, "Katrina, you are safe! You will stay with me until we get through this."

Katrina responded, "You don't know that! These are very dangerous men, and they can find you anywhere."

Rod reassured her, "They have not been successful so far, and now they know we are on to them!" He then reassured her with "We are not letting up, and we will get them."

Katrina, still in fear, replied, "I hope so before they kill me."

Rod then said with confidence, "That's not going to happen." The two then exited the vehicle in the hotel parking lot, and Rod put his arm around her and hugged her with a look of endearment. In that moment two shots rang out, one shattering the passenger window and the other lodging in Rod's shoulder. Rod immediately pulled Katrina to the pavement in an effort to cover her from being hit. Two more shots were fired from a black unmarked sedan flying by and driving out of the lot onto the adjacent street. Rod was holding his shoulder and grabbing for his cell phone and at the same instance questioning, "Katrina, are you hit?"

She, with tears flowing down her face, blurted out, "No, I am OK, but you are shot!"

Rod in a panic reiterated, "I am OK. We need to get help."

Katrina screamed, "We are not OK! You see? They can find us anywhere."

Rod dialed with one hand while still holding his other arm over the wound and calmly requested backup and explained the situation. Then within minutes police cars arrived, and an emergency medical vehicle shortly thereafter. Katrina had her hands covering her mouth as the EMTs escorted Rod to the rear of their unit. The police were trying to comfort Katrina and at the same time secure some explanation of the incident. Katrina just kept staring at Rod and ignoring the officers' questions. Rod turned toward her and winked as if to indicate it would be OK.

Gus Lucas, now very suspicious of Nicholas, called Victoria back and questioned, "Have you heard from him?"

Victoria, sitting at the table in the truck stop with a cup of coffee and the truck driver across from her, in an irritated voice replied, "No, I haven't, and I am going to find him and kill him myself!"

Gus in a calm but demonic tone added, "No, you leave that to me. I will take care of Mr. Musso." In that moment, the large garage door began opening as one of his henchmen was pushing the button for the automatic chain lift at the appearance of the first truck arriving and waiting to enter. Gus, with somewhat of a surprised look, turned and watched the large carrier, with smoke being ejected through the vertical exhaust, enter the warehouse.

Nicholas was now standing in the rear of the motel as truck number five, or the last truck, pulled in and stopped. Nicholas, with a slight smirk and half grin, walked over and instructed him to drive the rig to Cortez Street and McClelland Avenue in Laredo, park it, and walk away. In that moment an individual who was very thin and lanky, with a Hawaiian shirt not tucked in, walked quickly but calmly and attached explosives and a remote igniter device to the underneath of the truck. Nicholas handed the driver a handwritten, addressed note and reiterated to him to park and walk away. He then handed him a small case of money and impressed upon him not to fail him as he was being watched. The driver responded, "Si, Señor," and drove away.

Gus Lucas was now watching as his men and workers were checking out truck number one and the contents, as they were concerned about the quality of the contraband, when a truck horn blared outside the warehouse. The door was once again raised, and truck number two rolled through the door and into the warehouse. Gus now had an expression of wonderment. He then called Victoria on the phone and informed her of the two trucks that had arrived and questioned, "Has Nicholas returned?"

Just as she began to answer, she noticed Nicholas walking through the entrance of the truck stop restaurant. She then blurted out, "He is walking in as we are talking!"

Gus then told her, "Get to the bottom of that and call me back."

Just as Nicholas walked up to the table, he noticed Victoria's purse placed beside her on the adjacent chair to her left. He walked up behind her as she was hanging up and dropped his cell in her purse. He then kissed her on the head as she turned to view him. She immediately began screaming at him, "Where the hell have you been?" She then continued without hesitation, "Why wouldn't you answer your phone? What's going on?"

He then in a defense replied, "I am sorry. I was checking all the exits, trying to locate that first truck, and I threw my phone in your purse before I got out of the car when we saw the fire.

Victoria then looked in her purse and found the phone. She then in exasperation said, "Shit, father wants to kill you, and he thinks you were planning this!"

The local police walked into the truck stop and were directed toward Victoria and Nicholas. Nicholas took charge and addressed the police officer and explained, "Yeah, we had a trailer of air conditioner compressors highjacked."

The police officer questioned, "Did you get a description of the highjacking truck?" Nicholas then described it as a white Peterbilt that had hitched the trailer and headed east toward Beaumont. The officer then, in a cynical tone, stated, "That should be easy to track down!" He then requested Nicholas's driver's license, and Nicholas, with a look of concern and loss, defended himself with "I don't have it, and I was just explaining to my wife over there"—as he pointed to Victoria—"I lost my wallet."

The officer then demanded, "I need some identification here!" Victoria, listening and with an eye roll, handed over her license.

CHAPTER 17
THE EXPLOSION

Rod, now in the ER, sitting on the edge of a table covered with sterile paper, was being ministered to by a nurse. She was placing a bandage over his treated shoulder wound. Katrina was seated outside the ER door, waiting patiently and sobbing. Rod then walked out and explained, "That was a warning by Lucas."

Katrina then, in a low tone, said, "Yes, but they always know where we are all the time."

Rod then, with an aggressive demeanor, responded, "I agree with you, Katrina, but now we are going to put an end to our complacent attitude and outsmart them."

Katrina then tilted her head in a show of disbelief and exclaimed, "Yeah, sure."

The large door opened again at the warehouse, and truck number four pulled in and parked. Gus then called Victoria back, and she immediately blurted out, "Nicholas is here, and his phone was in my purse. He put it there during the fire."

Gus then questioned, "Did he catch up to the stolen trailer?"

Victoria answered in exasperation, "No, he never caught up to them!"

Gus in frustration impressed on Victoria, "I will find out who is behind this, and that person will pay!"

Victoria, in acknowledgement of his aggression, took a deep breath and replied, "I understand, and we will get them."

Gus then questioned, "Trucks one, two, and four have arrived, and I understand number three is missing, but where is five?"

Victoria then stated, "Well, five should be here soon."

Rod, driving with his arm in a sling, looked over at Katrina and pulled up to another hotel and not the Residence Inn. Katrina then asked, "What are we doing here?"

Rod sighed and explained, "Well, we are not going back to a location they obviously know about!"

Katrina, in a sarcastic tone, quickly interjected, "I think Mr. Lucas always knows where we are, and he probably knows we are here now."

Rod then questioned, "Did you notice we didn't leave in my car but in this different-color car, and we exited through a side door?"

Katrina then sheepishly said, "Yes, we did go through that side door, and you are right, we are in another car." She then finished with "How do you know there were no spies at the emergency room?"

Rod ended with "I don't know, but I am trying to fool them in every way I can!" Katrina took a deep breath and remained silent.

THE EXPLOSION

Victoria and Nicholas were now driving up to the warehouse at Cortez Street and McClelland Avenue in Laredo. They entered through the side door, and Gus Lucas walked up and hugged Victoria but gave Nicholas a suspicious look and questioned him: "You never found anything?"

Nicholas, somewhat indifferent in his demeanor, responded, "You know, Gus, I didn't find anything, and your suspicions of me really piss me off!" Nicholas then furthered his defense with "You got me out of jail to help you, and you haven't trusted me since you brought me here!"

Gus then grunted and cynically stated, "You left my daughter in that truck stop!"

Nicholas again in defense answered, "I didn't know who or what I was going to find if I caught up to them. If they had started shooting and your daughter got hit? What would you have thought then?"

Gus, realizing he might have been mistaken, apologized to Nicholas as he responded with "You may be right, so let's all cool off and all settle down." He finished with "We need to find out who took two of my trucks."

Nicholas, still appearing frustrated, stated, "I need to go get a drink."

He then headed for the door, and Victoria jumped in with "I will go with you!"

Nicholas quickly retorted, "No, you stay with your father. I need a moment." Victoria then tilted her head with a look of disappointment but backed off as she turned and looked at Gus. Nicholas then headed to the door and departed. He then walked quickly to the vehicle and noticed truck five driving up, and he turned and nodded his head at the driver. The tractor-trailer rig pulled up in front of the warehouse, and the driver descended from the cab and looked both ways, as if to observe if anyone was watching him, and then walked down the street.

Rod and Katrina were now kissing passionately beneath the sheets in the hotel room. Rod calmly explained that he really needed to go back to the jail and follow up on the arrest of Gus Lucas! Katrina, now very nervous, complained to Rod, "I cannot stay here alone again, Rod!" She then added, "You left me for too long, and they will find me and want to kill me."

Rod then followed with "I will only be gone for about two hours, and I will call you every thirty minutes to check on you, but you can't come with me."

Katrina, in fear, again expressed her concern: "Rod, I am scared. Please don't leave me." Rod then reassured her that he would call and have an officer placed outside the door. Katrina, worried, stated, "Suppose they follow the policeman here?"

Rod, as he dressed to leave, then convinced her with "No, I will call for a plainclothes officer to come and guard you."

Katrina realized his determination, settled back, and in a defenseless response said, "OK." Rod kissed her and then pulled his cell phone out and made the call as he exited the room door.

Nicholas, after driving around the block, now sat staring at truck number five parked in front of the warehouse. He looked down at his cell phone and dialed in a code. The truck exploded, and the diesel tanks burned in high, flashing flames. The roll-up doors

THE EXPLOSION

were completely blown in as Nicholas was attempting to see if there was anyone rushing out or moving within the warehouse. No one, after only minutes, appeared from the wreckage of the smoke-filled destruction. Nicholas at first wanted to check and see if Victoria was alive but restrained himself from exiting the vehicle and instead drove off. He heard the wailing of sirens in the distance, as someone must have called the police and fire departments.

Rod arrived back at the Laredo police station and heard about the explosion. He questioned a local officer as to the location. When he heard Cortez and McClelland, an alarm went off in his mind, as he remembered that locale and warehouse all too clearly. He then turned around and jumped back into his car and accelerated out of the parking lot. Within minutes, he drove up to the warehouse and watched the firemen shooting the water in an attempt to get the fire under control and police lights flashing while officers flagged off the area. Rod then parked and immediately departed the vehicle, pulling his badge out. He ducked under the border tape and flashed his badge to the guards keeping spectators and news people away. Rod tried to enter the warehouse and noticed that two men lying on the floor near the main pull-up doors appeared dead. He then saw Victoria already being assisted by medics. He next viewed Gus Lucas lying on a table, also being checked, as his coat was burned and his shirt opened, while a medic was taking his pulse. Rod then turned and noticed the three trailer rigs. He then went over to the back of one of the trailers and climbed up to the level of the tarp covering and lifted it up and observed the contents. He then jumped down and stared at

THE RESOLVE

Gus Lucas, who now saw Rod, but couldn't react. Rod then went over to the head officer and mandated, "Cuff them all and place a guard on anyone requiring medical attention." He then instructed the officers to seize the trucks and ordered that no one be allowed to leave the premises if all was safe.

The fire chief came up and assured Rod, "All is secure here, providing nothing else is scheduled to blow!" He then continued, "That rig outside had explosives attached and appears to have been detonated right where it was parked." Another fireman, standing with a bag of the illegal contraband in his hand, displayed it on the table and in an excited tone blurted out, "That trailer is filled with the same stuff out there like in here!"

Rod, now attempting to put all the pieces together in his mind, contemplated that someone else was sabotaging Gus Lucas and his organization. The question was who. Rod called Brad Kingsworth, still in Laredo, and explained, "Well, someone else handed us Gus Lucas and his dope on a silver platter."

Brad then, with a surprised look on his face, questioned, "What the hell is going on?" Rod gave him all the details, and Brad immediately instructed Rod to hold everyone in place as he was having a task force headed that way with transportation to transport all of them to the jail. He wanted guards surrounding the warehouse. Brad concluded with "This may be the biggest bust of my career."

Rod then called Katrina, and she answered instantly, "Rod, where are you?"

Rod then told her, "Calm down. I have Gus Lucas and his whole gang in custody right in front of me!"

Katrina pessimistically responded, "Rod, he will get away and come and kill me this time."

THE EXPLOSION

Rod then assuredly stated, "Not this time, Katrina. We have got him with his coke in hand." He then explains that she could turn on the local news and watch, but he would be a little while rounding these bad guys up and booking them into jail.

Katrina now in fear questioned, "Where are you going to take them?"

Rod then answered, "Right here in Laredo, to the jail, before we transport them to a state prison, but we have to arraign them first." He then closed with "I have to go, Katrina! It will take me a little while, so be patient," and he then clicked off his phone and turned to look at the handcuffed Gus Lucas. Katrina turned and, with both her hands on her face, stared into the room mirror, and tears streamed down her cheeks with deep contemplation. The medical staff was still addressing all the wounded while the fire department checked for additional fires and gas lines. Rod then headed out the door to investigate the blown-up truck.

CHAPTER 18
A DEADLY SHOT

Ten minutes passed, and Brad Kingsworth walked through the blown-open lift door and addressed Rod: "Well, I guess you are just plain lucky that this all fell into your lap?"

Rod then, with a worried look on his face, responded to Brad: "Yeah, maybe, but who blew this place up and set Lucas up?" He then added, "Is there more cargo, and where is Nicholas Musso?"

Brad, now also with a look of concern, interjected his thoughts: "Maybe Mr. Musso double-crossed Mr. Lucas?" Brad then began to turn to Gus Lucas across the room and stated, "At least, Rod, you have part of the package, and he can't deny possession of this massive confiscation and disruption of drugs flowing freely into this country." Brad's task force team arrived, and he instructed them to round all Gus's people up and transport them back to the Laredo jail. The coroner was pronouncing the two henchmen that were blown up at the door dead, and one of the task force members was now escorting Gus Lucas to the exit. Brad turned and couldn't help himself as he looked Gus Lucas in the eye and blurted out, "I guess, Mr. Lucas, this is all the hearsay and witness we need!"

Gus Lucas grunted, "I want my lawyer!" The agent jerked Gus Lucas by the arm and walked him out the door.

A DEADLY SHOT

Rod was now investigating the burned, blown-up truck at the entrance and saw part of the detonator still hanging from the trailer rig. He instructed one of the agents to bag it as evidence and get flagging around this truck and trailer rig. He yelled out, "I don't want any of this cargo touched or moved until we have counted every bag here!" Rod then walked around to the cab and looked in through the blown-out driver's door. In the same moment, Victoria was being rolled out on a gurney with her hands cuffed to the frame as the medic loaded her into the EMT unit with flashing lights. A light rain from the overcast day began to fall as the EMT unit pulled away. Rod stared at Victoria as she also turned and gave a hard look back at Rod with her mouth mumbling indistinguishable words. Rod rolled his right eye upward and shook his head with an I-can-only-imagine look.

The scene back at the Laredo jail was somewhat chaotic as each of the task force units and police cars pulled up and unloaded the guilty parties and escorted them through the crowds of media and cameras flashing. Loud voices came from the police officers yelling for the media to get out of the way as they walked each suspect through the now-building crowd outside the jail. The rain began to fall as the shoving of people was now making the arrest difficult. Five minutes later, the vehicle now arriving with Gus Lucas in the rear seat pulled up and parked as close as possible to the prison door. The agent got out of the door on the passenger side and opened the rear door, where Gus Lucas was assisted in exiting the unit. When the agent had retrieved Lucas and walking him to the jail entrance, lightning flashed, and the sound of thunder rumbled heavily in the dark sky. In that moment a small-frame individual wearing a gray-colored raincoat and hoodie walked up behind the agent and Gus Lucas and raised a hand with a 9-millimeter handgun and fired two shots into the back of the head of Mr. Lucas. Gus Lucas fell to the ground, dragging the agent with him as he grabbed his arm. The shooter stared for a moment, dropped the handgun, and started to run as another agent rushed and grabbed the perpetrator by the arm and wrestled the assailant to the ground. The agent pulled back the hoodie as Rod Tillman ran up to see who it was, and the face now exposed was Katrina's.

Rod, with a defenseless look, questioned Katrina: "Why? We had him! You were safe! Why?"

Katrina, with tears in her eyes, said, "He would have beat the system and gotten out and then killed me and my family, and I could not let that happen!"

The rain was now heavy over Rod as water dripped from his face, and he just shook his head with such a discouraged look. The agent lifted Katrina up by the arm and placed handcuffs on her wrists. Another officer in uniform leaned over Gus Lucas, checking his pulse and his chest, looked up at Rod, and shook his head. The officer then responded, "He is gone, sir!" Rod stood in the cold rain as it dripped from the brim of his hat, and he watched as the officer walked Katrina to the jail. He looked up at the floodlights that glared across his face and mumbled to himself out loud, "She is right, and that may be her defense."

Brad Kingsworth was back in the jail front office, questioning, "What the hell is going on out there?"

In that moment Rod walked in, dripping water from his face and hands, then answered Brad, "Lucas is dead!"

Brad replied, "What? Who? What are you talking about?"

Rod then, after a deep breath, answered, "Katrina just shot Gus Lucas in the back of the head and killed him!"

Brad then questioned, "But why?"

Rod then again informed him, "Katrina shot Lucas because she felt he would escape the charges and the system and get out of jail and kill her and her family."

Brad thought for a moment and then, in a defense gesture, puckered his lips and raised his eyebrows and casually made a point: "I can see how she would think that, Rod." He then, with another pinch of the lips, continued with "I think she could appeal to a judge or jury with a self-defense pleading, and she would beat the system!"

Rod then looked at Brad with a more confident expression and interjected, "Maybe you're right, Brad! I think she could beat it with a self-defense plea!"

The sky was partly cloudy in West Texas with the sun shining down on the front of an older-model Peterbilt. The white hood of the truck and the hood ornament glistened. The driver softly hummed with a toothpick hanging outside the edge of his mouth. Nicholas Musso was driving truck number three, headed toward California. He had a load of cargo for sale if he could just make it to San Diego. Nicholas noticed a typical countryside motel outside San Antonio with a sign saying "Welcome, Truckers" posted on the marquee at the entrance. He steered the large truck-and-trailer rig onto the paved parking area and stopped within walking distance of the single glass door of the lobby. He departed the truck, reaching for his wallet as he approached and grabbed the door handle and entered. Nicholas maintained his expressionless look and demeanor as he asked, "Do you have a single king on the ground floor available?" The crusty old receptionist guy replied "We sure do" as he handed Nicholas the key to room 107. Nicholas then relocated his rig near the room entrance and out of the way of other vehicles. He entered the room and turned on the TV, looking for news. He first worried that Gus Lucas might come looking for him, but later, after watching the news in his room, he learned otherwise when they flashed the murder of the drug kingpin Gus Lucas. He had a sigh of relief on his face. However, his thoughts wandered back to Victoria, as there was no mention of her demise in the newscast.

The scene now drifts back to Victoria being ministered to by a nurse practitioner at the Laredo medical facility. She was still handcuffed, now to the emergency room table. Her face was filled with extreme anger, as she had just heard of her father's murder at the police station. In a very low tone, as the nurse turned away, she exclaimed, "I am going to get you, Nicholas! I am going to find you and kill you!"

The attending nurse heard the angered voice and addressed the cuffed prisoner: "Excuse me—are you in pain?"

Victoria, with a witchlike expression, responded, "More pain than you and these medical phonies could possibly treat!"

CHAPTER 19
REVENGE

The judge's gavel hit the bench desktop as the gray-haired sixty-seven-year-old made his declaration. Katrina, standing at the defense table with her court-appointed attorney, intensely listened to the judge's ruling. Rod Tillman, FBI agent, sat in the last bench, near the exit, at the rear of the courtroom, with his left arm on the backrest and his right hand gripping the seat edge as he listened to the judge's decision. The key words he heard in the judge's explanation, as he continued to address the defense, were these: "Although homicide is homicide, there is an obvious case to be heard that there was some justification, due to the fact that the victim, Mr. Gus Lucas, had made two attempts on the defendant's life." He then granted Katrina a conditional suspended sentence to include house arrest under the custody of the FBI until a hearing date could be set.

Katrina, somewhat relieved that she was not being brought to jail, turned and hugged her attorney as she cried out in a soft voice, "Thank God!" Rod stood and waited for Katrina to walk toward him. She turned to Rod and, in a rush motion, headed down the aisle, tears streaming down her cheeks, to grab Rod. Rod, still attempting to maintain his professional decorum in front of the judge, hugged Katrina and patted her on the back. Katrina, realizing his posture, looked up at Rod and, in a sheepish tone, stated, "Thank you!"

Rod tilted his head and, in a sympathetic voice, responded, "I think we need to get out of here and get you a drink." Then both turned and walked through the big double doors of the courtroom, and Katrina, in one motion, turned and caught Rod's right hand.

Once outside the courthouse, Rod walked toward the black assigned sedan he had parked in the lot, still holding Katrina's hand. Upon reaching his vehicle, he opened the passenger door for Katrina, and then heard the loud, shrill screeching sound of a black SUV heading toward them. Rod turned as he closed the passenger door and observed the SUV's windows going down and two automatic weapons blasting directly at them. Rod reached in his coat for his shoulder weapon but had to run and duck for cover as a spray of bullets penetrated in a pattern all along the right side of his vehicle. He then raced to Katrina, who was bent over in the seat, and he pulled the door open. He reached in and noticed Katrina was unconscious. He yelled, "Katrina, Katrina, are you OK?" Katrina didn't respond and fell toward Rod. Rod turned Katrina toward him, and a stream of blood began to soak her blouse. Rod, realizing she was shot, checked her neck for a pulse and yelled into his police radio intercom, "I need an emergency vehicle and police support to the Laredo courthouse ASAP. I have a shot female victim and need immediate attention!"

The police response was "Unit en route. Do you have a pulse?" and Rod answered, "Got a pulse, but I am losing her." Rod continued to hold Katrina and searched her chest for the entry wound and realized the bullet had pierced in the vicinity of her heart and probably punctured her lung. He applied pressure to the entry wound and tried to awaken her. He didn't want to move her in fear of harming her conditions. The sirens were wailing as the emergency unit pulled up, and the EMTs exited their vehicle and approached Rod. They pulled Rod from the vehicle and begin administering first aid to Katrina. They removed Katrina from Rod's sedan with an oxygen mask strapped to her face as they transported her via a gurney to the emergency transport unit. The unit pulled out with sirens blaring, and Rod stood in the parking lot with his hands on his face.

Rod jumped back into his bullet-ridden vehicle and pulled out of the lot and headed to the hospital. Rod called his chief, Brad Kingsworth, and informed him of the shootings. Brad exclaimed, "It is Gus Lucas's fucking gang retaliating for her shooting Gus!" He then added, "We need to get protection for Katrina at the hospital! I am sending four agents there now and requesting police guards at the entrances of the building."

Rod answered, "Thank you, Brad. I am headed there now."

Brad then questioned, "Did the judge release her?"

Rod then replied, "Yes, he did, with probation and therapy."

Brad, excited, said, "Rod, they must have had an informant in the courtroom!" Brad then questioned, "Do you remember anyone else in the courtroom?"

Rod answered, "Well, there were a few spectators, but I wasn't looking for any notable participants." He then finished with "I guess I need to get my head out of my ass and pay attention for Katrina's sake."

Rod pulled up to the emergency entrance of the hospital, exited the vehicle abruptly, and ran into the emergency entrance and up to the information desk. He flashed his FBI credentials and demanded to know where they had taken Katrina. The female attendant, somewhat annoyed by Rod's anxious and demanding demeanor, addressed Rod: "She was taken to surgery, and you cannot go in there."

Rod, staring at the attendant with a disgusted look, responded to her with "Are you going to have the police remove me?"

The now wide-eyed attendant, realizing she had pissed off the FBI agent, rescinded and calmly explained, "Sir, the doctors are working to revive her, and you cannot interfere with that process, as that would only cause a problem for the woman who was shot."

Rod, although concerned, understood he needed to cool it. He then went to check and see if any of Gus's goons were roaming the hospital and if the FBI agents assigned by Brad were in place. Rod realized that the agents were situated at strategic locations, looking for unsecured personnel or guests roaming the halls of the hospital. Once he felt the area was secure, Rod went out to his vehicle to check the shot-up panels and search for bullets inside the cab. Rod noticed that Laredo police units were now stationed at the front and rear of the hospital. He then called Brad back and informed him of the ordered patrol coverage at the hospital. He then inquired, "Do you think, Brad, that the attack was to make an impression or was a vindictive message by Gus Lucas's daughter, Victoria?"

Brad, understanding Rod's concern, expressed in a sympathetic fashion, "Rod, who knows, but I don't think it was a message, and yes, they intended to kill both of you for the demise of Gus Lucas."

Rod then came back with "So they are not going to stop until they succeed?"

Brad then answered, "Rod, obviously we got to get them all!"

Rod then returned to the hospital and headed to the waiting room for surgery. He sat in a chair isolated from others, waiting, and stared at the hallway doors to surgery. In that moment, a doctor came through the door but addressed a couple waiting to hear about an individual who was in grave condition. The doctor informed the couple that the person was out of surgery and was satisfactory for now. The couple both looked relieved and thanked the doctor as the surgeon turned and returned back through the doors. Rod then surveyed with his eyes the entire waiting room, and he noticed one individual with a gray flannel sport coat and a black shirt who looked completely out of place. Rod continued to observe the individual's eyes and movements. The heavyset male appeared to be in his fifties and was of Spanish descent, with long, slicked-back hair. It almost seemed apparent he could not be an assailant. No organization attempting to take out an FBI agent would be that stupid, but then again, the world is full of idiots. Rod watched as the individual went to the coffee machine and two of the agents walked up to him and questioned him and then spun him around and handcuffed him behind his back. Rod shook his head and spurted out, "No way!"

Victoria Lucas, in a prison jumpsuit, with her hair pulled back into a ponytail, sat at a table in the visitation hall of the Webb County Detention Center across from a Spanish man in a black suit. Victoria stared directly at him and questioned, "Have you taken care of Katrina and that FBI cop, Felipo?"

Felipo, Victoria's first cousin, being the son of her father's brother, Marco Lucas, responded to Victoria, "Well, we attempted to take both of them out when they came out of the courthouse, and Katrina is in the hospital, but we didn't get the cop."

Victoria, with a hard stare, angry and tight-lipped again, stated, "So, you accomplished nothing, but can you tell me where Nicholas is hiding?"

Felipo, with a look of failure, assured Victoria, "No, but I will find him!"

Victoria, now with an expression of total frustration, told Felipo, "Find him and put him in a secure private area, and get enough money to bail me out of here!"

Felipo apologetically replied, "*Si*, Victoria, I will take care of everything."

—ɯ—

Rod was standing in the waiting room as the surgeon, still masked, walked toward him and pulled his mask off. He looked at Rod and, with a half smile, stated, "She is going to make it. She lost a lot of blood, and the bullet did pierce her lung, but we were able to get it out."

Rod anxiously questioned, "Can I get in to see her?"

The surgeon responded, "Well, she is still in recovery. Maybe let her rest, and tomorrow you can visit."

Rod, realizing the foolishness of his request, replied, "You're right…tomorrow," as he turned and headed toward the elevator. He, now with the anger emotions creeping back into his mind, pulled out in the new car rental, as the bullet-ridden sedan was back at the station as evidence. He called the station desk on his cell and requested the location of Victoria Lucas, who was being held on numerous counts related to drugs and even as an accomplice to murder.

The desk sergeant replied while scanning his computer screen, "She is being held at the Webb County Detention Center. Anything else?"

Rod, contemplating his next move, answered, "No, that will be all, Sergeant." Rod then flipped the wheel and turned up the next street, heading for the detention center.

Sitting in the interrogation room, Rod waited for Victoria with his FBI badge hanging out from his topcoat pocket and his visitor's pass around his neck. Two female officers escorted Ms. Victoria Lucas into the room. Her beauty, obscured by the prison attire and lack of makeup, still glistened in her dark Latin eyes and high cheekbones. Her emotions exploded as she entered the room and yelled at Rod, "You're the bastard that arrested my father and let that bitch shoot him!"

The two women guards corralled Victoria and sat her down across the table from Rod. Rod sat calmly with his cool demeanor and, in a low tone, addressed Victoria: "Let me look you in the eye and politely lie to you...I am sorry for your loss."

Victoria screamed back at him, "Fuck you, fuck you, you, you son of a bitch...that's my father you're talking about!"

Rod, again in a calm demeanor, informed her, "Ms. Lucas, let's cut the shit! He murdered a lot of people and imported a lot of drugs into this country." He finished with "Such are the risks!" Victoria, now silent, stared at the floor, and Rod again interjected, "One of those people he tried to murder on three occasions is Katrina, and she is now fighting for her life at this very moment." Rod continued, "I am here to make you a deal, Ms. Lucas. If there are any more attempts on her life at the hospital or anywhere, I will be coming after you, but that not being the case, you may have a more pleasant stay in our accommodations!"

Victoria retorted with tight lips, countering his deal with "You want a deal? Here is the deal...with all your computer surveillance technology wherewithal, find Mr. Nicholas Musso and discreetly inform me. Then two of your problems will be resolved!"

Rod, with his top lip pinched in the bottom of his mouth, stared at Victoria and requested the guards. The women guards escorted Victoria out of the room. Rod sat and contemplated Victoria's request as he also wondered about the whereabouts of Mr. Nicholas Musso. He then stood and told one of the guards still remaining at the door, "Tell Ms. Lucas I will be back in touch."

Rod exited the prison and returned to his vehicle. He connected with Brad on his cell phone and advised him, "Victoria is very volatile and announced her revenge intentions toward Katrina for the murder of her father."

Brad answered, "Well, you're not surprised." He then reassured Rod, "We have guards all around the hospital and outside the intensive care section."

Rod then turned his attention when he addressed Brad with "You know, she brought up one concern that still has me wondering."

Brad inquired, "What are you talking about?" Rod then explained, "She wanted us to persist in our efforts to locate Nicholas Musso." He then finished with "And I got to tell you, Brad, I am curious about his whereabouts myself."

Brad, with a look of questioning on his face, said, "I agree—we need to find him."

CHAPTER 20
THE COSTELLO CARTEL

Nicholas Musso was standing in the hazy sun in the middle of a used-car parking lot in Emeryville, California. The haze was caused by the last of the drifting fog from San Francisco Bay. Emeryville was just across the Bay from San Francisco, and the dealership lot full of used cars marked with prices on the windshield faced West MacArthur Boulevard. The location was an excellent marketing front, being situated near the I-580 turn ramp. Nicholas was waving his arms in an effort to make a sale to an attentive prospective buyer. Nicholas appeared almost out of character, being usually of a quieter demeanor. He had been able to sell a third of his stolen contraband to a dealer in the Los Angeles area but decided to store the rest in the San Francisco Bay locale and remain obscure for a period of time. He utilized some of the cash to move across the Bay to Emeryville and purchase the dealership, which he named Big Bob's Used Cars. Nicholas realized that his anonymity was his sole concern. If Victoria should discover his location, she would waste no time in contacting the local underworld for his demise. The car dealership was a perfect cover not only for appearing as an ongoing business in this area but also because no one would suspect Nicholas's personality of being that of a used car salesman.

Rod, back at the hospital, checked in on Katrina, who was now out of recovery and asleep in a regular room. Rod, sitting in a hard-backed chair, reached for his buzzing cell phone and answered in a low tone, "Yes."

The voice on the line was Victoria at the Webb County Detention Center. She informed him, "Since you are obviously aware of four of the loaded trucks, I am letting you know there was a fifth truck that was never found. I think Nicholas drove away in it, but what I don't know is where he went!"

Rod puckered his lips and in his typical tone responded, "Thank you, Ms. Lucas. That will help us in maybe finding him."

Victoria then blurted out, "Don't forget our deal, Mr. FBI!"

Rod then retorted, "What deal, Ms. Lucas? We haven't made a deal yet!"

Victoria then, with spite exuding from her eyes, interjected, "This is true, so we are still at square one, and everything is what it is!"

Rod, understanding her line of thought to be referencing threats on Katrina, explained sharply, "I assure you, Ms. Lucas, we are not at square one because we are aware of your attempts on Katrina's life, and although nothing is off the table, any such interim aggression will certainly bring on hard consequences." Then Rod ended with "Have a good day, Ms. Lucas" and clicked his phone off. Rod pondered the call and wondered how she had obtained his cell phone number and why she was so anxious for the FBI to locate Nicholas, who had obviously escaped with a truckload of their contraband.

Nicholas Musso, as he sat behind his desk in a disarrayed office, scribbling on a notepad, heard a door slam just outside the building. He peeked through the blinds of the covered window and saw two men exit a black SUV. They appeared to be of Latino descent and were wearing short sleeves with exposed arms tattooed from their wrists to forearms. They approached the steps, walked up on the stoop, and then entered. Nicholas looked up, realizing they did not look like prospective car buyers but rather messengers. Nicholas reached under his desk for a clip-ready 9-millimeter neatly positioned and placed his hand on the grip and finger on the trigger. Nicholas questioned, "Can I help you?"

The taller of the two spoke first: "Are you Bob?"

Nicholas nodded and answered, "Yes, I am Bob."

The Latino, in broken English, demandingly said, "Our boss wants a meeting with you to discuss some business about your recent sales."

Nicholas, sensing they were not there to assault him and releasing his grip on the gun, sat back and responded, "First who is your boss, and what business is he wishing to discuss?"

The taller one again explained, "Let's just say he is an important man in California, and he has an offer for you that may be very profitable."

Nicholas now understood this all had to do with his recent sale of the powder and that the local cartel had become curious about the source and quantity. The question that came to mind was this: Was this the concern of competition or a new source for their buyers who must be taught a lesson of respect by the local establishment? Nicholas then asked, "Where does your boss wish to meet?"

The obviously more outspoken Latino handed Nicholas a note with the name of a restaurant and an address. The Latino again spoke: "Our boss asks if 8:00 p.m. tonight would be convenient for you."

The other Latino now openly smiled and with an obvious accent repeated, with now a laugh, "Yes, convenient! Our boss wants to know if it's convenient!" The rhetorical use of "convenient" obviously amused the second Latino but gave Nicholas a sense that the boss was obviously intending for the meeting to make a point that their territory was being invaded without approval.

Nicholas ended with "Tell your boss that I accept and will be there at 8:00 p.m." The two Latinos, satisfied with their mission, walked out and drove off. Nicholas, now nervous over the possible exposure that could signal to Victoria back in Laredo, decided he must maintain his disguise to ensure his concealment and safety. If Victoria discovered his existence and locale, she would definitely team up with Costello in his demise.

—⁂—

Now on his way back to the Laredo police station, Rod pulled out his cell phone again and called Brad Kingsworth. He, in an anxious demeanor, told Brad, "Nicholas is on the run, and he's driving the fifth truck loaded with powder!"

Brad, with an expression of surprise, answered "Whoa." He paused and then again continued with "Where do you think he would be headed, and did he know about the explosion at the warehouse?"

Rod then immediately replied, "I am starting to think he is responsible for the explosion and now has some valuable product to sell!"

Brad then questioned, "Well, Rod, do you think Nicholas felt confident with the planned explosion at the warehouse and doesn't know about Katrina's assassination of Mr. Lucas? Because he wouldn't want the cartel on his ass."

Rod, with a deeply concerned expression, began expressing his thoughts out loud. "If he did blow everybody up and take off, then he would still be on the run from the cartel."

Brad then responded, "Yeah, you are right, so he is headed as far as he can get from here in any case." Brad then finished with "We need to get out a nationwide APB on Mr. Musso."

In the restaurant, Nicholas was now sitting across the table from Mr. Ramon Costello, a notorious western cartel head who operated out of Los Angeles, California. Also seated at the table were two obvious henchmen of Mr. Costello dressed in slick, sheened black suits, one with a dark-colored shirt and a shiny silver tie. He was obviously of Latino heritage, while the other, with light brown hair combed uniformly to the back, was possibly of mixed Italian descent and was wearing a black dress shirt and no tie. Mr. Costello was a man in his midsixties wearing a dark knit shirt with an open collar and a light-colored sports coat and was now staring at Nicholas. Nicholas, in his usual light multicolored Hawaiian shirt and no coat, waited patiently for Mr. Costello to speak first. Costello asked Nicholas, "Mr. Bob, would you like something to drink or eat?"

Nicholas replied, "I will have a shot of Jack Daniels." Costello waved his hand at the waitress, and Nicholas looked up at her, holding two fingers together, and said, "A shot of JD, no ice."

THE RESOLVE

She responded, "Yes sir."

Costello now addressed Nicholas in a serious tone: "Who are you, and why are you undercutting my business in San Francisco?" Nicholas had commenced to answer when Costello cut him off with another question: "Where are you getting your supply?"

Nicholas, now mentally deciding on exactly how much information he wanted to divulge, responded, "I came from New Orleans, and I am getting out of the business and selling what I have left."

Costello, now leaning back in his chair, wiped his mouth with his bare hand and stated, "Yes, but you sold over a million and a half of your product to some of my best customers!" Costello then leaned forward, with both his elbows on the table and hands again near his chin, and instructed Nicholas with "You cannot come to my house and give candy to my children and I not know!" Costello then questioned, "You understand?"

The waitress, at that moment, placed in front of Nicholas his shot of Jack Daniels. Nicholas, not experienced in the territorial control of each cartel, realized he could not demonstrate his ignorance and shook his head in agreement. He then replied, "I understand, but I was trying to unload my last of the product and just buy my used-car dealership and retire."

Costello again looked hard into the eyes of Nicholas and in a forgiving demeanor told him, "I forgive you for your indiscretions, but surely you know, after being in this business, that there are rules, and if you break the rules, it cost you!"

Nicholas, with a look of anticipation, and now waiting for the other shoe to drop, asked, "And what do you, Mr. Costello, think is a fair price for breaking the rules?"

Costello sat back and contemplated a figure in his head and, with his eyes now shifting back and forth toward his two henchmen, spurted out from the side of his mouth, "Five hundred thousand." Costello then looked over at Nicholas to observe his reaction.

Nicholas, somewhat shocked at the rule-breaking fine, answered, "That is a third of what I got!" Nicholas then again explained, "I have already spent most of that on the dealership." Nicholas, now looking at the two henchmen and their satisfaction in the deemed punishment of their boss, stated, "Can you not have a little mercy for one of our own now retiring?"

Costello answered quickly, "You break the rules, you pay the price!" Costello, now getting up from the table, mandated to Nicholas, "You will have payment tomorrow at your dealership at noon, and my two associates here will be there to pick up the package." Costello stood up, turned, and headed toward the door as Nicholas rose in unison with the two henchmen.

One of the henchmen, the one without a tie, sarcastically informed Nicholas, "Mr. Costello expects for you to pay the tab and tip the lady well! She is one of his favorites." The henchmen then caught up to Costello and walked out the entrance. Nicholas, frustrated with thought of paying this cartel asshole this amount of his profit stash, which he had acquired and orchestrated with the Gus Lucas cartel, sat back down and ordered another drink.

Rod, now driving up to the Laredo police's local compound yard housing the trucks from the Gus Lucas warehouse raid, parked adjacent to a large warehouse. Rod, after exiting his vehicle, approached one of the large trucks that had not been damaged in the explosion and inspected the trailer and photographed with his phone several views of the whole unit. He then walked over to the officer managing the yard and questioned, "Do you have the tarp that covered this trailer when it was brought into this yard?"

The officer, somewhat nonresponsive, replied "Yeah, they are folded in that shed over there" as he pointed to a metal storage building across the compound. Rod had begun walking toward the building when the officer added, "Ah, it's locked."

Rod, now aggravated by the officer's laxed attitude, turned and questioned, "The fucking key, genius?" The officer, detecting the frustration in Rod's tone, reached in the guard door and grabbed the key. Rod, shaking his head again, approached the building, unlocked the door, opened it, and saw the tarp. He snapped another picture on his phone and then departed. He, now sitting in his vehicle, phoned Brad Kingsworth and informed him that he inspected the trucks at the Laredo police compound and took pictures. He then suggested that they needed to contact all truck scales and truck stops along I-10 from Florida to California and see what had been recorded. He informed Brad, "We need to show photos of Nicholas Musso and these truck profiles to support our APB bulletins across the country."

Brad, now biting his lips, and with an expression of deep thought, answered Rod, "I agree, and we need to let your friend Victoria Lucas know what we are doing and maybe get her support."

Rod, shaking his head, returned in comment, "Yeah, why do I feel like I really don't give a shit what that bitch feels?"

Brad then immediately retorted, "Well, think of Katrina's safety, if nothing else."

Rod, nodding in agreement, responded, "I agree, and I will let her know."

It was 11:45 a.m., and Nicholas sat behind his desk at his dealership as he awaited the arrival of Costello's goons to collect the briefcase of money placed on top of the desk. Five more minutes passed, and a black sedan pulled up in front of Nicholas's office. The same two henchmen from the previous night's meeting exited and walked into Nicholas's office. The Latino first addressed Nicholas and questioned, "Hello, Mr. Bob, do you have a package for Mr. Costello?" Nicholas looked at the floor and then looked up at both men. He pulled his 9-millimeter from under the desk and shot both men without speaking—two direct shots in the temple. Each man, with a look of surprise, dropped to the floor.

CHAPTER 21
A RUN FOR IT

Nicholas, now still staring at the two men dead on the floor, got up from the desk and looked out the office window to see if anyone or other salesmen might be approaching the door. He then dragged both men into a back adjoining room and locked the door. He next went to his wall safe and removed all his cash and packed it into the briefcase on the desk. He noticed one of his car salesmen coming toward the front door, walked out, and interrupted his entrance by asking him to go pick him up a sandwich at Subway down the street. He handed the salesman a ten-dollar bill. The salesman agreeably turned and headed back out. Nicholas returned to the back room, unrolled a roll of plastic wrap, and began wrapping it around each of the dead men.

Rod now, after driving up to the hospital and heading up to the entrance, walked in through the automatic doors and approached the elevators. He pushed the button and continually scanned the surroundings, observing everyone in the lobby for any unusual characters. The elevator doors opened, and Rod, along with two women, entered. Rod exited on Katrina's room floor and headed toward her room. He again took notice of everyone along the hallway, including the stationed security guards in place to protect Katrina. He knocked on the door and entered, noticing the tubes and life support equipment surrounding her hospital bed. She looked up at Rod, and a tear dripped down her cheek. Rod, in a low tone, asked, "How are you feeling?"

Katrina, in an effort to respond, murmured, "I miss you."

Rod grabbed her hand and squeezed lightly and replied, "Take it easy. You are safe, and I am staying close." She squeezed his hand back and drifted off into sleep.

The darkness was overcoming the San Francisco metropolitan area, and Nicholas now dragged each of the now plastic-wrapped men to the front door of the office. He flipped off the lights to the back section of lights highlighting the used cars uniformly aligned in two rows. Nicholas walked out to check for any onlookers in the immediate vicinity before transporting the corpses. He next opened the trunks of two separate used vehicles that he self-determined were not going to be sold anytime soon. Nicholas then loaded each wrapped body over his shoulder and carried them and deposited them separately into each vehicle. Nicholas, after returning to the office, flipped the back display light back on, grabbed his briefcase and a duffel bag of his clothes, and departed the office, locking the door behind him. He picked out a newer vehicle on the lot and threw his bag and the briefcase in the trunk. He then climbed into the driver's seat, started the engine, and drove off, heading toward I-580.

THE RESOLVE

Rod, with a disgusted look on his face, again sat across the table from Victoria Lucas. He informed her, "We have placed an APB out on Mr. Nicholas Musso, and we are investigating all truck scales and truck stops along I-10 from Florida to California."

Victoria, with a pleased expression, questioned, "Do you think you will find him?"

Rod returned with "Oh yeah, we will get him, but he will not be under your control."

Victoria, now with a Cheshire cat look, and in a cynical voice, stated, "Now, Mr. FBI, you are never knowledgeable of our control measures!" She then looked Rod straight in the eyes and closed with "It would be good for you to keep that in mind with Ms. Katrina."

Rod's whole demeanor now shifted, and his eyes become very enraged on Victoria as he exclaimed in a low tone, "You might keep in mind that you are the one incarcerated and presently under our control." Rod stood up, turned, and called for the guard to let him out as he exited the room.

Nicholas pulled his vehicle up to a small warehouse on the outskirts just off I-580. He unlocked the padlock on the two large double doors and swung them open to view the large truck still loaded with the remainder of the product. Nicholas cranked up the diesel as the exhaust smoke billowed up inside the warehouse, and he pulled the truck forward outside, allowing room to drive the car back into the space. Once the vehicle was parked, he opened the trunk and removed the duffel bag and the briefcase. He then placed everything into the cab of the truck and closed the large doors and locked them. Nicholas climbed back into the still-running truck and pulled off.

He looked both ways as he made his turn onto the entrance road and waved his hand in a half upward motion and mumbled, "Hell, I got to find another town!" A rear view of the truck showed the exhaust now blowing hard as he accelerated again toward I-580.

Rod drove up to the front of the Laredo Medical Center off East Saunders Street as Katrina was being transported in a wheelchair by an attendant. Rod parked at the patient exit door and jumped out to greet her, but first, in a moment of caution, he scanned the adjacent parking area for any possible invasive characters that might try again. He smiled at Katrina, who looked up at him with a half smile, and a sparkle in her eye glistened as he rhetorically asked, "How are you doing?"

Katrina, in a loving but sarcastic tone, answered, "Glad to see you."

Rod assisted Katrina into the passenger side of the plain white sedan and then again surveyed the parking lot before getting in and driving off. He turned to Katrina and informed her, "Look, I am taking you to my hotel room so you can clean up and we can get something to eat, and then we have to make a plan to remove you from any possible future involvement that threatens your life!"

Katrina then turned, in some obvious aching and pain, and responded to Rod, "I am never going to be safe without you."

Rod looked first at her, realized this was not the time to have a conversation about their long-term relationship, and then looked back at the road, remaining silent. Katrina looked to her right, staring out the passenger window with a sad expression as she in turn came to the realization of what his silence obviously meant.

THE RESOLVE

—⋘—

Nicholas was now driving along I-580 into Tracy, California, and this was decision time as he approached Interstate 5, the north-south corridor through California. Nicholas must now decide whether he was going north to hide along the West Coast or heading south to I-10 and then east to Florida. The thoughts of both areas to live in had been dangling in his mind since he left Emeryville. He needed first a place to sell his contraband in small quantities without being noticed in the drug world, and more importantly a location off the FBI's radar. He resolved to veer north on I-5 toward Sacramento, then up through Oregon. Nicholas determined in his mind that the Gus Lucas clan had already thrown him to the wolves and an all-out computer search was probably being broadcast on the FBI website. The truck stops around the country were no doubt already networked for any observances of him with a description of him and his truck.

—⋘—

Rod escorted Katrina to his room, holding her arm as he opened the hotel room door, and she entered and sat on the edge of the bed. She noticed Rod had gathered some of her clothes and personal items on the dresser next to the flat-screen TV. Rod showed her in the room closet various articles of clothes and dresses he had purchased. He blushed and took a deep breath when he blurted out, "I had the girls at the station help me with the sizes and basically tell me what to get that you might like."

Katrina, appreciating his obvious awkwardness and attentive gestures, smiled and said, "You are so kind and thoughtful, but I am still scared, and I think you are wishing that I were somewhere out of your life."

Rod, now truly understanding her fear and what he had obviously conveyed in the vehicle, now interjected, "Katrina, I care about you a lot, but this is serious, and it exposes you to some very dangerous people. Your safety has to be my first concern. My feelings have to be placed on a back burner for now."

Katrina, now comprehending his commitment to protecting her, smiled and shook her head in agreement.

Rod's cell rang, and it was Brad Kingsworth. Brad immediately explained, "Rod, we got a report on a double murder in California, and it has Nicholas Musso's DNA all over it!"

Rod responded, "Brad, I am getting Katrina secure, and she needs to eat something, and then I will make it down to the station."

Brad replied in a matter-of-fact response, "Yeah, well, make it soon, Rod, 'cause I am planning on heading back to Houston today. I've had enough of Laredo and the locals for a while."

Rod then returned with "I hear you, Brad. Just give me an hour to take care of her, and I will be there."

Brad, looking at his watch on his wrist, murmured back, "OK, see you in an hour."

—⚊⚊—

Nicholas pulled his rig into a small truck stop along an out-of-the-way exit off I-5 just north of Sacramento and parked between two on-site eighteen-wheelers to remain somewhat obscured from sight. He headed into the café and pulled his baseball cap down over his forehead, disguising his appearance. He then sat at a far end table in view of a large TV behind the bar. The news was just coming on, and a waitress at the same instant asked, "Sir, may I get you something?"

Nicholas, looking at the limited single-card menu, told her, "Yeah, give me this large burger with everything on it and some fries."

The waitress then questioned, "Would you like cheese on that burger?"

Nicholas replied, "Yeah, yeah, whatever."

She turned and walked as she was writing on a pad. Nicholas looked up just as the news commentator was showing his used-car dealership and while describing the murder scene interjected, "It is believed the double homicide is connected to the cartel underworld." The newsman continued with "We have a possible suspect" as Nicholas's photograph appeared on the screen, and the commentator ended with "He was an escapee from the Texas State Penitentiary at Huntsville, known as the Walls Unit, six months ago."

Rod and Katrina finished eating the sandwiches he had obtained at a local café as he explained to her, "Listen, Brad is heading out to return to Houston, and I have to go meet him before he leaves."

Katrina complained, "You are going to leave me here alone?"

Rod impressed on her, "I have to, but I will be right back."

Katrina, with much concern in her expression, took a deep breath and pointed out, "At the hospital you had guards protecting me!" She questioned, "Am I safe here?"

Rod handed her a cell phone, and he instructed her, "Take this phone and keep that door locked; I have my own key, and I will call you in thirty minutes." Katrina moaned and grabbed Rod's hand. Rod closed with "Be strong for me, and I will be as quick as I can." Rod walked out the door and quickly headed to the elevator.

Rod pulled up to the Laredo police station, jumped out of his vehicle, and proceeded straight to one of the back offices, where he greeted Brad with "Hey, what we got on Nicholas Musso?"

Brad reacted with "Glad to see you too, Rod." Brad then looked down at a paper on the desk and interpreted to Rod, "Well, someone saw Nicholas putting something like a body in the trunk of a vehicle in a used-car lot known as Bob's Used Cars in Emeryville, just on the outskirts of San Francisco!" Brad then added, "But wait—it gets better! The used car lot is owned by Bob, a.k.a. Nicholas Musso."

Rod exclaimed, "Whoa!"

Brad then further explained, "They next checked all the trunks and found another body, and now they have an APB out on Nicholas!"

Rod then inquired, "Do they know who the murder victims are?"

Brad responded, "It appears that Nicholas took out two of the Ramon Costello cartel gang members."

Rod tightened his lips and raised his eyebrows and commented, "I guess Nicholas has more than the police and FBI on his tail, now with the Lucas and the Costello cartels both wanting a piece of him!"

—⚅—

Nicholas, now finishing his burger, looked up as two state troopers walked into the truck stop restaurant and ordered coffees at the bar counter. Nicholas pulled his cap farther over his forehead as the waitress walked up and asks, "Will there be something else? We have a great apple pie."

Nicholas looked up and in a low tone replied, "No, just a check." She tore off the ticket and handed it to him. Nicholas looked at the tab and observed the amount of $11.80. He pulled out a twenty-dollar bill, handed it to her, and said, "If you take care of that for me, you can keep the change.

She smiled and responded, "I will, and thank you."

Nicholas then stood, eyeing the troopers, who had not noticed him, as he walked out the entrance and headed to his truck. He knew that if he pulled his truck out now he might be noticed, and he just could not expose himself now. He needed a diversion to remove all possible attention being directed at him.

CHAPTER 22
CABIN IN THE PARK

Nicholas was sitting in his truck, unnoticed, between two eighteen-wheelers with container-enclosed loads. His mind contemplated a plan to escape from this truck stop. Nicholas then waited until dusk and slipped out of the cab and strolled around the various trucks now parked and saw a flatbed with two fuel cans placed in a rack behind the cab. He looked around to observe all individuals milling around in the vicinity. He discreetly slipped the cans out and walked back to his truck. He next went and paid cash for filling both cans with gasoline and then returned again to his truck and waited. He sat and quietly observed when everyone was settled down within the parking lot. He then picked out three tractor-trailer rigs that were isolated and unmanned. He carried the two cans of fuel and placed one can at the rear of the first truck and opened the fuel cap of the diesel tank. He then pours half the can of gasoline into the tank and then poured a trail of fuel to the next truck. He emptied the first can into the second truck and then continued with the second can of fuel, leaving an extensive trail of fuel. Nicholas finished the second can with the third truck. Evaporation being a concern, he lighted the first trail, which flamed a stream of fire to the first truck. Nicholas ran back between the parked trucks as the massive explosion of the first sent flames to the second and the third. The diesel was now burning, with extensive flames rising up above the lot and metal flying up in all directions. Nicholas climbed back into his truck and drove back to I-5 as he looked in his mirror at the glowing reflection of the rising flames.

Victoria received a hearing and was charged as an accessory to racketeering and drug smuggling as she claimed innocence in her father's business. However, bail was set, and Cousin Felipo bailed Victoria out. Victoria, via the news media, was now aware of the whereabouts of Nicholas and his recent association with the Ramon Costello cartel. She detected that Nicholas had been attempting to sell his stolen product and that Costello got wind of it and probably sent his goons to take him out. Costello's network had more surveillance in this business probably than the FBI. Victoria tried to get a message to Costello through the underworld communication network via the connections of her father, Gus Lucas. Victoria's name and cell phone number finally appeared in an envelope in front of Ramon Costello. The note read, "We have a common enemy, and if I get my piece, I will give you yours! If you agree, please call."

Nicholas, driving the truck north on I-5, was concerned about state troopers being alerted to his location now because of the truck. He did not want to cross the California-Oregon state line, so he decided to pull off at the Redding, California, exit. Redding had a population of about ninety-two thousand and was situated approximately halfway between Sacramento and the Oregon state line and might be the perfect hideout until the FBI and drug cartels calmed down. Nicholas pulled into the first fast-food outlet and parked. He got a burger and drink and sat while he thought about his future. He still had sufficient cash to hole up for a month or two while he waited for his popularity—he was now a fugitive from the FBI, plus the drug cartels wanted his life—all to calm down with time.

Rod drove back to his hotel and immediately headed to his room, knocked, and opened the door as Katrina was sitting on the edge of the bed with a look of fear in her eyes. Rod hugged her as she murmured in pain and squeezed his neck. Rod then informed her, "Victoria is out of jail," and Katrina quickly responded, "She is going to find me and kill me!"

Rod exclaimed, "No, she is not, because I made a deal with her that I would find the man she wants dead more than you." He continued with "She realizes we have the means to find him anywhere in the United States."

Katrina curiously asked, "You are going to find this man and give him to her to kill?"

Rod then answered, "No, but she thinks we will, and that gives us time to put you in the witness protection plan system."

Katrina then anxiously complained, "But I want to stay with you, and what about my family?"

Rod, realizing her concern, reiterated, "Victoria is not her father and wouldn't take the time to track down your family, as her immediate rage is for Nicholas!" Rod reassured her, "We will relocate your family as a precaution, but we have to get you in the witness protection plan."

THE RESOLVE

—⟫⟪—

Victoria received a call from Ramon Costello, and she answered, "Mr. Costello?"

Costello answered, "Ms. Lucas?"

Victoria began with her introduction: "Mr. Costello, I am Gus Lucas's daughter, and I am sure you have heard that my father was murdered at the Laredo police station while in custody?"

Costello again responded, "Ms. Lucas, I am aware of everything you have told me, but who is this used-car salesman, Bob, and where did he get this much product to come and sell in my territory?"

Victoria, ready to reply, provided an explanation. "Mr. Costello, his name is Nicholas and not Bob, and he stole that product from us and blew up our warehouse, hoping he would prevent me and my father from ever catching up to him!" She then ended with "I want him, and I want to look him in the eye before I kill him!"

Costello, in an exhausted mannerism, exhaled with a "Whew" and then complained, "Well, Ms. Lucas, how do I explain to the families of my two men he murdered and stuffed into those car trunks?"

Victoria then stated as a resolve, "How about, Mr. Costello, if when we catch him, we take the product he didn't sell and pay a share to compensate the two men's families before I kill him?"

Costello ran his fingers over his lips while considering her offer but came back with an ultimatum as he informed her, "Here's my deal, Ms. Lucas: you pay me $100,000 for each man, and I go away, or I go find him, kill him, and take it all."

Victoria unhappily responded, "I need a day to think about it. Can I call you tomorrow at this time?"

CABIN IN THE PARK

Costello mandated, "No, I will call you at the same time" as he clicked his phone off.

———~m~———

Nicholas, after finding a cabin in an isolated recreational park area outside Redding, parked his truck behind the cabin and covered it with a large tarp, with plans to find an unused, discreet storage warehouse location and rent a car in the morning. He purchased some groceries from a nearby store and placed a steak on an outside grill and noticed a very sexy woman in jeans and a sweatshirt jogging along the wooded trail behind the cabin. She stopped, turned, and greeted Nicholas with "Hi, you just move in?"

Nicholas looked up, noticed her lean body and long hair, and with his usual demeanor, addressed her interest with "Yeah, need a break from the rest of the world, and this place seems perfect." The woman picked up on his obvious shyness and, being intrigued again, continued the introduction with "Well, I am the next cabin over, and my name is Beth."

Nicholas now walked over toward her and, curious about her sudden interest, responded with "I am Jake from California. Are you visiting, or do you live here permanently?"

She, now staring into his large brown eyes, explained, "No, I am from Oregon, and I come here every year for a month." Nicholas tipped his large cooking grill fork toward his head and nodded with "Glad to meet you!"

Beth smiled and as she turned to leave, saying, "Maybe we can get together for a glass of wine if that's OK with you?"

Nicholas half smiled and again nodded in agreement. "OK!" Beth then jogged off.

THE RESOLVE

—ᴍ—

Katrina sat up in the bed and saw Rod asleep in the chair, covered with a blanket. She exclaimed, "Rod, Rod!"

Rod, startled, sat up and questioned, "Katrina, you OK?"

Katrina responded, "Yes, but I need you in this bed now." She expressed again, "Please, come and get in this bed and hold me! I am not hurting, and I don't break!"

Rod got up and approached the bed. He unbuckled his belt and dropped his pants and climbed under the covers with Katrina. He looked into her eyes and kissed her, then nestled into her neck and caressed her body close to him. Katrina smiled and softly stated, "I need you, Rod!"

—ᴍ—

Victoria was now sitting in a small warehouse office approximately one block down from the burnt warehouse along McClelland Avenue in Laredo. Cousin Felipo approached her and reported, "Victoria, we are very low on product and need to bring more in from Colombia for our customers."

Victoria looked up at Felipo and sarcastically responded, "I am well aware, Felipo!"

She then bit on the pen in her right hand and thought aloud with "If I can find Nicholas and that last load, I am sure he still is holding the bulk of that container and hiding the truck."

Felipo then questioned, "Are you going to make a deal with Mr. Costello?"

Victoria, still in thought, was coming to the full resolve that if she gave Costello $200,000, he would still try to find Nicholas, kill him, and take all of what was still on the truck. She then blurted out, "No, I don't think I am going to make any deal with Mr. Costello."

Coincidentally, her phone rang, and it was Costello. Victoria picked up the phone, and Costello questioned, "Ms. Lucas, do we have a deal?"

Victoria then pensively questioned, "Mr. Costello, what's to keep you, after I give you the $200,000, from going after Nicholas and stealing the rest of my product?"

Costello, in an effort to show honor, but in a suspicious tone, answered, "Ms. Lucas, we have a code of honor in our business to maintain!"

Victoria immediately returned with "Mr. Costello, I don't know you, and if there is nothing else I learned in this business, I did learn there is no fucking code of honor."

Costello then, in a matter-of-fact expression, responded "Then the race is on, Ms. Lucas!" He clicked off, and Victoria, with an evil stare, slowly put her phone on the desk.

Brad Kingsworth, now back in Houston, received a call from Rod to question him about Katrina being placed in the witness protection program. Brad explained, "Rod, she is on probation but still involved as the guilty party in a murder investigation. I agree Lucas was a piece of garbage, and she saved the government a ton of money in taking him out, but she is still in this case, and we cannot put her in witness protection at this time. Hate to say it, but we are her witness protection."

Rod rolled his eyes and complained to Brad, "You got to help me with this! I need a more permanent place to hide her until this is over. I need an apartment, a house, or somewhere out of the mainstream. This hotel room is too vulnerable and easily accessed!"

Brad then thought and stated, "I will see what the budget will allow us, and maybe we can set her up in a suburb residential rental that keeps her hidden." Brad then added, "You will have to limit your comings and goings."

Rod instinctively understood the point and answered, "I hear you, Brad."

Nicholas and Beth, becoming more acquainted, were now sitting outside his cabin sipping wine as the grill was smoking, with that barbecue aroma drifting in the air in the tranquil wooded scenery. Beth, increasingly becoming more interested in Nicholas and his past, poured forth with questions. Nicholas, wanting the companionship but without the research into his history, dodged the interrogation by constantly changing the subject. Beth, in her tight jeans, pullover sweater, and long brown hair flowing over her shoulder, again continued in her investigation as she questioned, "So you sold your business in Louisiana and drove out west searching for something different?" She then extended her interest: "Did you leave any family back in Louisiana?"

Nicholas then released with "Yes, my mother, and a brother."

He then went silent, and Beth, noticing his restraint, again inquired, "No previous marriage or children?"

Nicholas then reluctantly interjected, "Yeah, I had a wife, but she died, and we never had any children."

Beth then, with concern, responded, "Sad."

Nicholas instantly, in an effort to change the conversation, questioned, "How about you—you ever been married?"

Beth then elaborated, "Yes, my husband was a victim of brain cancer and died two years ago in Portland. We came out here every year, and I am still coming and reliving the experience of this beautiful country."

Nicholas got up from the wooden chair, a permanent fixture outside each cabin, and said, "Let me check our steaks!"

Beth, still in memory, looked up with sadness in her eyes and remained silent for the moment. Nicholas noticed her whole demeanor had changed from the initial joyous, full-of-life personality to now a calm and almost sad expression. He attempted to cheer her up with a wave of his hand in a gesture as he expressed, "Look at the two of us in this beautiful outdoors, talking about the sadness of our pasts, when we should be enjoying the present and hopefully some happy times in the future!"

Beth then looked up at him and raised her glass of wine as she then toasted, "To the future!"

CHAPTER 23
A NEW LEAD

Rod went and visited with Victoria's probation officer and got an address on her local operations and then drove to her office on McClelland. Looking out the plate glass window, she observed him walking from his parked sedan across the street straight to her front door. He walked in to face her sitting behind the wooden desk, and she greeted him, "You missed me, Mr. FBI, and wanted to see what I looked like not in prison-assigned orange garb with no makeup?"

Rod half smiled as he viewed Victoria dressed in a long black dress, with her hair pulled up, wearing dangling silver earrings. Her complexion was smooth and had that slight Latin tan, her lips a bright, shiny red. In an inquisitive manner, Rod asked, "I came to see if you and I still have a deal with Katrina."

Victoria, also with a half smile, responded, "So Katrina means something to you more than just being the obvious assailant and murderer of my father?" Victoria now returned to her serious look and tightened her jawline and, thinking Rod was emotionally involved with Katrina, improved her position as she replied, "I expect you, Mr. FBI, to keep your part of the deal, and I urge you to step up the search for Mr. Musso because the Costello regime wants him as bad as I do. So there are time limitations, as you can see!"

Rod, then realizing her cocky tone was because she thought she was in control, decided to bring her back to reality with "Ms. Lucas, you are a convicted felon out on probation, and we can easily change your accommodations and dress code, so cool it with the threats. If I even suspect a threat on Katrina, I will find you!" Rod then turned back toward the door as Victoria blurted out, "She killed my father. That fact will always be with me, and I have lots of connections in or out of your prison!"

Rod, aware of her anger, stopped, turned only his head, and puckered his lips to say "I get it!" and went out to his vehicle. Victoria, now standing, stared at him all the way until he got in his vehicle.

Brad called Rod on his cell and informed him, "Rod, we got a location on Nicholas Musso."

Rod questioned, "Where, and who informed you?"

Brad then answered, "You know we have several fugitive cases we are working on, Rod? It was by chance, while the guys in California were tracking down a suspect in a homicide that had crossed state lines from Oregon, that they noticed a truck-and-trailer rig that matched the one in the Lucas case traveling through Redding, California. They followed up on it and checked the computer files and did a match. The driver fits Nicholas's description." Brad then finished with "They want to know if we want them to grab him."

Rod replied, "No, I want to get him, but I need them to keep someone on him until I can get there, because first I need to place Katrina somewhere safe before I fly out there!"

The night was overcoming the cabin as the light gleamed through the windows across the front entrance and as the crickets and all the forest creatures of the night seemed to chime in together. Nicholas and Beth embraced while staring into each other's eyes. They passionately kissed and began stripping their clothes off and fell onto the sofa. Now totally in the nude, Nicholas admired every inch of Beth's very streamlined and in-shape smooth lines. Although still carrying a hint of guilt from a sense of betrayal to the honor of her late husband, Beth was still enjoying a possible distraction from her ongoing pain of the past. However, from a distance, well hidden in the brush, a scope with crosshairs centered in on both of them through the window. They made love and hugged while Nicholas was totally engulfing Beth's body out of view.

The morning sun was bright and reflecting on Rod's sunglasses as he carried Katrina's bags out of the hotel to his vehicle parked under the portal at the front entrance. Katrina, having trouble with one of her high heels, hobbled behind, questioning, "Where are we going, Rod?"

In his totally obvious nondomestic demeanor, Rod threw the luggage and assorted bags from Katrina into the back seat and opened the passenger door for her. He demanded, "Katrina, please get in. We need to get away from here quickly!"

Katrina again, as she positioned herself in the vehicle, asked, "Where are we going?"

Rod then explained, "We have rented a house in the suburbs for you, which will keep you out of sight until we can sort everything out."

Katrina, still worried about the Gus Lucas cartel, questioned, "But they will still find me and try to kill me, Rod!"

A NEW LEAD

Rod assuredly tried to calm her down with "If you don't advertise and maintain a discreet way of life, they will not find you, and we will keep a constant watch, so relax." Rod then further explained, "I have to fly to California for two days and pick up a suspect that will hopefully stop all the attempts on your life."

Katrina then asked, "Who are you going to pick up? Are you going to leave me alone here?"

Rod responded, "Trust me, Katrina—you will be safe if you don't leave the neighborhood!"

Katrina continued to look down in concern. She then surprisingly looked up and stated, "I trust you, Rod, and I will do what you say."

—⚡︎—

The morning sun was now beaming through the cabin windows as Nicholas and Beth dragged themselves off the sofa, aching from the night of being embraced and not in their normal sleep postures. Beth spoke first. "Well, good morning, Jake."

Nicholas, still not totally adjusted to his new name, which recently was changed to Bob and now Jake, mumbled out "Ah, ah, good morning" as he searched for the bedroom door and the connected bathroom to relieve himself. Beth sat up, eyed a coffee pot, and covered herself in Nicholas's shirt, using it as a robe as she placed coffee grounds for percolation. She yelled toward the bedroom door, "Jake, do you have sugar and cream?"

Nicholas, staring at himself in the bathroom mirror heard and exited the bath and stood in the bedroom doorway and viewed, once again, her shapely silhouette making a shadow from the sunlight's rays through the window. He then told her, "The sugar and cream are in the cabinet to the left." Beth turned and saw him with his hairy chest and in his boxers, standing sheepishly and in dire need of a woman's care.

Victoria now decided to have Felipo follow Rod in the interest of seeing where Katrina was located and to determine if he had gotten a lead on Nicholas. Gus Lucas had a couple of officers in the Laredo Police Department as paid informants, but he had never provided Victoria with their names. Within moments of her discussion, Victoria received an anonymous call, and the informant expressed to her, "Look, your father was good to me, and so I am giving you this information only this once, because I owe him."

Victoria questioned, "And you are?"

The informant impressed on her, "You do not know me and won't, but what I tell you is a fact!" Victoria listened intently, and the informant continued, "They found Nicholas, and he is in a cabin on the edge of town in Redding, California, and we are done!"

The informant hung up, and Victoria smiled and then addressed Felipo as she instructed, "Felipo, I have changed my mind. I want you and Julio to book a flight to California and rent a car to bring someone back to me in the trunk!"

Rod did not realize after he booked a flight to Sacramento that he, Felipo, and his assistant, Julio, were all sitting in the Houston airport at the same gate, but not facing each other. The flight desk called for first-class ticket holders to board. Felipo and Julio stood in line to board, but Rod was flying the government-approved coach. He looked up from his iPad and half noticed Felipo and Julio and recalled some memory of having seen them in the past. When Rod came through the first-class section, he again eyed Felipo and Julio sitting next to each other, sipping champagne. Felipo's gray flannel sports coat and black shirt and Latin complexion placed his identity as someone, well, let's say not from corporate America. Felipo never noticed Rod and tried to adjust the video screen situated on the front headrest. Rod sat next to an attractive woman in her thirties, her legs crossed, as she tried to pull her skirt lower while noticing Rod's wandering eyes. Rod continued trying to place Felipo and Julio in his mind. In the meantime, he said hello to the woman next to him and opened his iPad.

Upon departure from the airplane, Rod headed straight to the Enterprise car rental desk while Felipo was already standing in line at the Alamo rental line, waiting to be assigned a vehicle. Felipo, being aware that Nicholas was holed up in a cabin outside Redding, headed up I-5 to investigate all the cabin rentals around the city. While just pulling out of Sacramento's regional airport, Rod called Brad to check on Nicholas and his place of residence, and he questioned, "Brad, do you have some information for me? I am on the interstate, heading to Redding."

Brad responded, "I am waiting on a call from the department now and should be able to give you a call back with the exact location shortly."

Beth and Nicholas now arrived in Beth's cabin, which exuded the charm of a woman's touch with the obvious display of feminine decor. Although feeling an extreme attraction to Beth and her very prominent controlling personality, Nicholas was also very aware of his awkwardness with the touch of class in her world. Beth, in an effort to calm his revealing tension, exclaimed, "Relax, Jake. I am not that fragile, and I do somewhat appreciate your nonaggressive mannerisms."

In an effort to appear comfortable, Nicholas sat at the table and parted with a compliment: "You have dressed this place up well—kinda makes mine look shabby!"

Beth, grinning, replied, "We will get yours in shape soon!"

In the same moment, a gunshot pierced through the kitchen window and hit Beth in the left shoulder. Beth, in total shock, looked at the blood spreading over her blouse, then fainted and dropped to the floor. Nicholas jumped from the chair and onto the floor to hold her. He grabbed a kitchen towel to stop the bleeding.

The perpetrator was now eyeing the crosshairs of his rifle through each window, trying to locate Nicholas. He edged close up to the cabin and yelled, "Come out, Nicholas, and I won't kill you." He reiterated to Nicholas, "Leave her, and she might live. I winged her to get your attention."

Nicholas was trying to revive Beth as she woke and felt the pain in her shoulder. She screamed at Nicholas, "What the hell is going on?"

Nicholas tried to calm her, and as he stopped the bleeding, he attempted to explain: "I didn't mean for you to get involved. I never thought they could find me here!"

Still staring in shock, Beth questioned, "Your name isn't Jake, is it?"

Nicholas looked down and confessed, "No, it is Nicholas!"

Beth then again asked, "So all this was a fake, a disguise?"

Nicholas immediately reacted, "No, no, I truly care about you, but I got to get them away from you." He then grabbed her cell,

A NEW LEAD

called 911, and gave the responder the address and her cabin number. He then dialed his recently paid-for cell phone number to maintain Beth's number.

Beth then sat up, holding her shoulder, and asked, "Where will you go?"

Nicholas responded, "I am not sure, but if I call you, will you answer?"

Beth shook her head yes and interjected, "Of course I will!" In the same instant, a 9-millimeter was pointed at the perpetrator's head and fired. Nicholas heard the second shot and tried to look out the window. The cabin door was kicked open, and Felipo stood with the gun in his hand as he demanded, "Nicholas, come with me, and you will live!"

CHAPTER 24
THE FIND

Felipo heard the sirens in the distance, and he noticed the truck-and-trailer rig behind Nicholas's cabin. He grabbed Nicholas, who was standing in the doorway, and questioned, "Where are the keys to the truck?"

Nicholas, realizing he was caught and any escape attempt would endanger Beth, handed over the truck key. Felipo pitched the key to Julio and instructed him, "Take the truck to Victoria!"

Julio, startled for the moment, questioned, "You want me to go now?"

Felipo shook his head and screamed at Julio, "*Si*, now, pronto!" Julio then ran toward the truck and cranked up the diesel and pulled out. Felipo yelled at Nicholas, "Let's go!"

Nicholas, now wondering if Felipo knew that Beth was wounded and sitting on the floor, decided to move quickly toward Felipo. Felipo, unaware that Beth's cabin was not Nicholas's cabin, pushed Nicholas to the car, opened the trunk, and told Nicholas to get into the trunk. Nicholas obliged and climbed into the trunk, and Felipo jumped into the driver's seat and pulled out as the emergency unit and police pulled up to the cabin. Felipo, thinking he had escaped the police, remained calm and drove away at a moderate speed. The police saw the glass window shattered, cautiously entered the cabin, and saw Beth on the floor. They called for the EMTs, who administered first aid to Beth. The police questioned her, wanting to know who shot her, while another officer saw the perpetrator shot in the head by the tree. Beth, contemplating that if she discussed anything about Nicholas she could get him murdered, decided to appear ignorant, as if the shot through the window were random. The police begin immediately interrogating and canvassing all the cabins. The EMTs transported Beth to the emergency unit as she noticed the police knocking on Nicholas's cabin door. She yelled from the gurney, "He is visiting his mother and not in!" The police moved to the next cabin, but to no avail. No one had heard or seen anyone shooting in the area.

The emergency vehicle pulled out, and Beth received a text from Nicholas: "Go to my cabin and get all my stuff and keep the briefcase full of money until I get back to you…I am safe in the trunk." Beth, not sure if she should reply, sent a thumbs up.

Felipo caught up to Julio and waved as he passed, holding up his cell phone out the window. Julio understood and showed him his cell phone. Felipo called Julio and told him to stay on I-5 to I-10, and then they would head east back to Texas. Julio responded, "*Si*, Felipo, but call me before you stop."

Nicholas, in the trunk, listening to Felipo's conversation, hoped Felipo would at some point come to understand that he needed to piss and needed water. Nicholas did not want Felipo to know that he had the cell phone. He received another text from Beth: "I am being transported to the hospital, and I think I am OK…I did not inform the police about you and told them you went to visit your mother."

Nicholas texted back, "Thank you, I will contact you when safe." Beth texted back with a heart.

Rod finally got a location on Nicholas via Brad, but it stated only that he was in a cabin on the outskirts of Redding and was not specific. Rod resolved there couldn't be many recreation parks with cabins in this remote area and researched all the rental cabins around Redding. He began to map out all the countryside cabins but was tired from the trip and first checked into a Hilton Garden Inn, and he then went to a sandwich shop adjacent to the Hilton Garden Inn and got something to eat. He thought about the fact that that Nicholas would use an assumed name other than his, but the truck might be parked adjacent to the cabin. Rod made a decision to retire for the night and get a fresh start in the morning.

Beth, four hours later, walked out of the emergency care wing of the hospital and took an Uber back to her cabin. She was anxious to go to Nicholas's cabin and retrieve all his stuff, including the briefcase full of money. She arrived and, although in extreme pain from the gunshot wound, went to Nicholas's cabin first. She, being aware of where he kept his hidden key in a pot in the bushes outside, grabbed it and opened the door. She immediately gathered all his personal items and saw the briefcase hidden under some of his clothes in the closet. She didn't open it then but carried two separate loads of all his belongings to her cabin. She then popped two pain pills and sat on the edge of her bed to rest. After five minutes of catching her breath, her curiosity overtook her, and she tried to open the briefcase, but it was locked, and there was no mention of a key. She wanted to text Nicholas back but was afraid of possibly notifying his captors of some vital information. She thought for a moment and remembered he did tell her that the case was full of money. She then exclaimed "Oh hell" and obtained a knife from a drawer and popped the latches. She opened the briefcase full of bound hundred-dollar bills. She exclaimed, "Oh my God!" Beth, now even more concerned, saw this was thousands and thousands of dollars and immediately assumed they were going to come back for this case. Beth made the decision she must leave in the morning for her home in Seattle.

Rod awoke in the morning and set out after grabbing a biscuit and coffee at the Hilton Garden Inn's in-house breakfast buffet. He went to each and every cabin in the Redding vicinity and finally saw on a register a single male from Louisiana registered under the name Jake Johnson and the license plate of a truck from Texas. He saw the cabin number and drove to the cabin. He went up to the door and knocked and knocked, but there was no response. He noticed a woman next door packing up to leave and walked over and greeted Beth with "Good morning, ma'am!" Beth looked up at him with her arm in a sling, and he asked, "Do you know the man in that cabin?" as he pointed to Nicholas's cabin.

She, being very nervous, said, "Not really."

Rod then showed her his credentials as he flashed his FBI badge. Beth, now completely frantic, did not know what to say but did not want to lie to the FBI and was suspiciously concerned that he must already know about the shooting and that was the reason for his

THE RESOLVE

questions. Beth finally stated, "There was a shooting here yesterday, and a man was killed!" She then added, "A stray shot came through my window and struck me in the shoulder, and that's why I am leaving!"

Rod, very aware of her nervous demeanor, asked, "Did you see any of the men?"

She, not wanting to be involved, replied, "No, I was shot and lying on the floor until an emergency unit showed up with the police."

Rod then asked, "Did you hear anyone talking?"

Beth commenced with her packing of her vehicle and again answered, "No, like I said, the bullet came through my window." She pointed to the kitchen window and added, "And it struck me in the shoulder!"

Rod then said, "Well, thank you, ma'am," and continued with "May I ask where you are headed to?"

Beth then hesitantly responded, "To my home in Seattle." Rod then asked for her address and a phone number should they wish to contact her.

Beth, now frustrated, wrote down her address and cell phone number. Rod began to turn but turned back and stated, "Sorry about your injury, and hope you have a safe trip home." Rod then headed out straight to the local police department.

Felipo pulled into a roadside motel in Arizona for the night and left Nicholas in the trunk overnight, but not before allowing him to take a leak and giving him a burger and three bottles of water. Felipo opened the trunk in the morning as Nicholas blocked with his hand the sunlight shining in his face. Felipo put a gun to his head and let him climb out of the trunk and escorted him to the hotel room and allowed him five minutes in the bathroom, but with the door open. Nicholas, aware that Felipo would shoot him without forethought, remained calm, walked back to the trunk, and climbed back in for the all-day ride. He texted Beth again and questioned, "Did you get everything?"

Beth, now driving back to Portland, excited to hear from Nicholas, texted back, "Yes, are you OK?" Beth then texted, "An FBI man named Rod Tillman came and asked questions."

Nicholas then texted again, "What did you tell him?"

Beth responded, "Nothing."

Nicholas answered, "Thank you."

Rod, now at the Redding Police Department, asked to see the body of the shot individual, expecting to possibly see Nicholas's body. However, when the morgue pulled out the drawer, Rod did not recognize the dead man. He then questioned the investigating officer, asking him if they had any information on who shot the man and if they had ever seen the man in the adjoining cabin. He then inquired about the truck, and all the answers were negative. Rod came to the conclusion that someone had come to kill Nicholas and took possession of the loaded truck of dope. Now, all he had to figure out was if it was locals or Victoria.

The night had arrived, and Felipo pulled up to the McClelland Street warehouse and drove right through the open double doors where Victoria awaited. Felipo anxiously jumped out of the vehicle and slipped around to the back of the car and popped open the trunk. Nicholas again covered his eyes from the brightness of the overhead lights and sat up. He then blurted out, "Hello, Victoria, you miss me?"

Victoria screamed at him, "You filthy son of a bitch! Did you bomb us and try to kill us?"

Nicholas slowly looked up at her and responded, "All we have been through, and you still do not trust me." Nicholas continued, "No, I did not bomb you, and when I got to the warehouse, the place had already been burned, and police were everywhere!" He then finished with "I thought I had better get that truck out of there!"

Victoria questioned, "What the hell were you doing driving that truck?"

Nicholas answered, "When I caught up to them off I-10, one truck was gone, and the other truck was being held up by probably the same group that set that bomb! I shot the guy and took the truck."

Felipo then angrily stated, "He is lying, Victoria."

Victoria, then retracting somewhat, raising her hand in an attempt to back up Felipo, asked, "So where is all my product?" She then added, "Before you screw up, I got a call from Ramon Costello, and he was pissed off that you invaded his turf."

Nicholas then, in a low tone, sarcastically, as he raised his eyebrows, eased out with "He is probably more pissed that I had to shoot two of his top goons."

Victoria, trying not to smile, again questioned, "So where is the stuff or the money?"

Nicholas then responded, "Two-thirds of the stuff is still on the truck, and I guess Felipo here"—he held out his hand toward Felipo—"took the duffel bag of all the money from my cabin."

Victoria then turned to Felipo, and Felipo immediately walked out to the truck and yelled, "Julio, did you get that duffel bag from Nicholas's cabin?" Felipo then turned to Victoria and defended himself: "Victoria, I told him to get the bag."

Victoria then turned in anger and sternly gritted out, "You fucking idiot! You didn't check?"

Felipo ran over to the truck and shot Julio while he was still sitting in the cab of the truck with his head out the window. Victoria then questioned Felipo, "Why did you do that?"

Felipo then, in an exploding fashion, screamed, "He was an idiot!"

Victoria calmly turned to Felipo with a curious look on her face and stated, "No, Felipo, you are the idiot!"

Felipo was now insulted, and his Latino anger controlled his emotion as he began to raise his gun a second time and point it at Victoria. Nicholas, in a leap from the trunk, reached out and grabbed Felipo by the neck as he twisted it, killing him instantly. Victoria, with an expression of amazement, looked directly at Nicholas and pleaded out, "You killed Felipo, my cousin!"

Nicholas, expressionless, again raised his eyebrows and defended himself with "Victoria, he was about to shoot you like he did Julio in the truck" as he motioned with his arm and hand to the parked truck.

Victoria was now feeling dreadful about Felipo but not sure whether to shoot Nicholas or not. She was thinking that Felipo did point the gun and Nicholas reacted on her behalf. She then questioned, while continuing to stare at Felipo's dead body on the floor, "How much money was left in the bag?"

Nicholas, realizing she would figure out how much he'd sold the stash for, decided to throw out a large number to be convincing and stated, "About a million bucks!" Victoria turned again with a questionable look. Nicholas then looked at her, raising his arms, and stated, "I had to live!"

Victoria then responded, "Obviously, you lived well, and what about the used-car dealership?"

Nicholas then answered, "I needed a cover, and I set up a diversion." He then continued, "If I could sell that, then you would get back another half a million dollars."

Victoria stood and glared at Nicholas with a total questionable look of doubt.

CHAPTER 25
TRUST FOR PRODUCT

Rod arrived back in Houston after connecting flights from San Francisco and walked into the main office. The receptionist at the entrance desk, a very attractive brunette, upon seeing Rod exit the elevator, peeked a look in her compact to check her makeup and, after turning slightly to expose her tan legs, greeted Rod with "Hello, Mr. Tillman, it's been a while since we have seen your face around here!"

Rod smiled as he glanced down at her name on a shiny brass plate: Helen McGuire. He responded, "And how are you, Miss McGuire?"

She sharply replied, "Helen, and the day just improved with your presence."

Rod picked up on the obvious flirtatious sentiment and, being well aware of the strict sexual harassment policies at the FBI, skirted the rules for a moment with "Helen, you certainly improved my day!"

Brad, now standing in the office doorway awaiting Rod's arrival with one hand on his hip, observing Rod's smooth display of alluring come-on lines, questioned, "Are you through?" Brad again reiterated to Rod as they walked together into Brad's office, "You know you are breaking all the written regulations about such things when you address the fairer sex with those suggestions of yours."

Rod immediately returned with "What suggestions, Brad? I just said hello and returned a compliment."

Brad came back with "Right, you know exactly what you are doing, but we have bigger issues at the moment!" Brad then interrogated Rod on his trip to California. "What's going on in California? Where are we with all this?"

Rod, with both hands on the back of a chair, shook his head and looked first to his left and then back directly at Brad and spewed out, "This whole investigation is fucked up, Brad."

Brad responded with a raised eyebrow, "What do you mean?"

Rod then began with "Nicholas Musso escaped from Laredo with a truck full of dope after the explosion of the warehouse, which I'm pretty sure he caused, but I can't prove that yet!" He then continued, "Then Nicholas sells some of the dope around San Francisco and acquires a used-car dealership." Again Rod looked to his right and, in a frustrated tone, finished with, "He obviously pissed off the Ramon Costello cartel by selling powder in their territory, and Costello sent two honchos to take out Nicholas, who, in turn, shot them and hid out at these cabins up north in Redding, California."

Brad, with a look of amazement at Rod's summation, questioned, "And now Nicholas is where?"

Rod immediately responded, "That's the big question."

—⚘—

Victoria, still somewhat despondent over Felipo's death, retreated to the back office at the warehouse as Nicholas followed her to the door. Nicholas, first remaining silent, then spoke up: "Victoria, I know what you are thinking, but this got all twisted up, and I knew I better save the one load, and then they shot your father."

Victoria, exasperated, shook her head then spoke in a low sad voice: "I hear you, Nicholas, and I want to believe you, and now I have no one else." She next, in a worried demeanor, complained to Nicholas, "We have another big problem, and that's how to get the rest of that powder from Colombia!"

Nicholas, now in a sympathetic mode and displaying an expression of sympathy, stated, "I can do it, and I am already experienced in the whole procedure!"

Victoria then looked up with a facial indication of total surprise and questioned, "So now you think you are totally back in my good graces and I should trust you completely?"

Nicholas, with a don't-give-a-damn look, responded, staring away, "Like you said, Victoria, you have no one else."

Victoria then answered, "Give me a moment here, Nicholas!"

Nicholas then received a text on his phone from Beth: "Are you OK?"

He texted back, "All good, will call soon."

Beth, now feeling somewhat unsure whether to text again but totally frustrated with not knowing and remaining in fear from both the FBI and possible unknown intruders, decided to get her anxiety out. She texted back, "Scared to death, and what do I do with this bag?"

Nicholas walked away from the back office and went into a restroom and texted back to Beth, "Hang on for now. Nobody is aware of you or the bag." He then added, "My perps are out of the picture, will explain shortly, relax!"

Beth, thinking, Sure, you are not the one holding the bag, texted back, "OK, but soon!"

THE RESOLVE

Rod, now sitting across a conference table from Brad, resolved, "We have to track Nicholas and that remaining truck, which is probably still full of dope."

Brad then questioned, "Where would they have gone with it?"

Rod then tried to analyze the whole situation with "Well, the Costello gang could have been the ones who caught up to Nicholas, but my money is on Victoria, as she is out of jail."

Brad raised his upper lip in some manner of agreement but, not totally confident, replied, "Yeah, but if you're wrong, then we got ourselves a whole new bucket of problems."

Rod, shaking his head slowly while in deep thought, expressed, "My gut tells me to go track Victoria, and unless you reject the idea, I am headed back to Laredo."

Brad sarcastically remarked, "Don't forget about Pocahontas in the teepee!"

Rod, realizing his conjecture toward Katrina, smiled and replied, "Got it!"

Two days passed, and Victoria, again thinking and saddened still over Felipo while pondering her next move, approached Nicholas, who had been bunking for the last two nights in a back room of the warehouse. Victoria knocked on the door, and Nicholas, with a white T-shirt and boxers, opened the door to Victoria, with her flowing hair glistening from the light, beaming from the backdrop, lips red and makeup outlining her daring eyes, questioning, "You plan on joining us today?"

Nicholas, now remembering how turned on he got and how Victoria always got his juices flowing, responded, "Didn't know we had any plans."

Victoria then answered, "Get dressed—I do have plans, and we need to get moving now before we run out of supply."

Nicholas, concerned and in a low tone, somewhat sheepishly asked, "So do you trust me again?"

Victoria, not sure "trust" was the right word at this time, made a judgment call and stated, "I am not convinced I can trust you, Nicholas, but the more appropriate word is 'need.' I need you right now!" She then added, "Remember, I am a felon and can't leave the country." Victoria looked at his physique as she scoped him up and down, with a thought of maybe later, and ended with "Join me in the front office in thirty minutes."

Rod drove up the street toward the new suburban residence of Katrina and carefully parked his vehicle across the street and two houses down from Katrina's new home. He waited in the vehicle for a couple of minutes to see if he had been followed and if anyone was milling about in the neighborhood. Once he was assured of the relative safety of his arrival, he exited the car and pulled out his cell phone and called Katrina to notify her of his approach. Katrina opened the door without appearing in the open space, and Rod walked in and closed the door. Katrina immediately threw her arms around his neck and exclaimed, "Oh my God, I have missed you!"

Rod replied, in his very matter-of-fact demeanor, "I missed you too, Katrina."

Katrina then, with her bright red glowing lips and glaring eyes, planted a kiss on Rod, who had an unexpected look on his face. Katrina then, with her arms still around his neck, questioned, "You are spending the night?"

Rod hesitated and then delineated, "Katrina, you have to understand—my attention to you at this time must remain professional, or we could jeopardize this whole case."

Katrina then, in a pleading tone, asked, "At least for dinner?"

Rod looked concerned but agreed, "OK, dinner, but then I need to leave."

Katrina smiled and left it with "We'll see!"

Nicholas, now at the airstrip which Gus Lucas had repeatedly utilized for his planes, discussed with two of Victoria's relatives the plans to fly to Colombia. The goal was to fill two of the matching twin-engine Cessna 206 planes with packaged product to bring back to sustain their customers until they could return for one large shipment, as previously attempted. Nicholas was curious about the question of whether this second plane was a decoy as before or truly a means to return with more product. The thought also crossed his mind that it was difficult transporting one small plane to the United States…so how was Victoria planning a double shipment? He then remembered how the authorities were all in, being well compensated by the kingpin, Gus Lucas himself. Did Victoria have the necessary clout "Ole Poppa" Gus had to get it done? Nicholas was now yelling at the related Latinos, "All right, let's get these birds in the air." He boarded the first plane and pointed his finger at the pilot wearing the ear-muffed headgear and exclaimed, "Let it rip."

TRUST FOR PRODUCT

The pilot revved up both engines simultaneously and positioned the plane in line with the asphalt-paved strip. Nicholas was peering out the window as he noticed the second plane not moving and Victoria arriving in a black sedan, exiting the vehicle, and running up to the plane and having a discussion with the second pilot. Nicholas was thinking What now and mumbling in a low voice, "Well, I don't think she is throwing in brownies for the trip!" Nicholas rolled his eyes with a suspicious look as the pilot throttled up and commenced down the runway.

The illuminated digital clock on the bedside table of Katrina's new residence had just ticked to 6:07 am as Rod raised his head while lying next to Katrina. He first, and very quietly, in an anxious tone, blurted, "Oh shit, this ain't good!" He then carefully slipped out of bed and pulled up his trousers and buttoned his shirt. He then grabbed his badge and holstered gun as he headed toward the bedroom door.

Katrina, now startled, opened her eyes and softly muttered out, "You really have weird hours, Mr. Tillman!" Rod stopped in his tracks, turned around, and bit his bottom lip as he softly responded, "Yeah, as I said, this isn't a great idea, the witness and the agent, well, you know."

Katrina, with a sleepy smile, looked at him and answered after a deep breath, "I don't even think the bad guys are out there waiting for you, much less your boss at this hour."

Rod, shaking his head in agreement, explained, "I got to go!"

Katrina slipped the covers up to her nose and stuck her hand out, waving goodbye.

THE RESOLVE

Nicholas and the Latino cousins, having arrived the previous evening, were now standing, the next morning, in front of the renovated storage warehouse that had been bombed. Nicholas, recalling his near-death experience, was looking around the compound as the newly assigned manager walked up and greeted them with "Hello, *mis amigos*. I was expecting your arrival." The manager then addressed Nicholas directly: "You are looking well, Mr. Musso!" Nicholas was not appreciative of the comments from the manager as he wondered if he had been involved in blowing him up.

Nicholas, with a halfhearted expression, replied, "Thank you. Is the stuff ready to be loaded?"

The manager, now aware of Nicholas's uncongenial expression, responded in a more serious tone, "*Si*, Señor, the forklift will load the pickup trucks, and we will help you load onto the planes." Nicholas then demanded, "Then let's get going, and we may get back before the sun goes down!"

Rod walked into the Laredo police station and retreated to the back office of the captain and questioned, "Have y'all had any reports of Nicholas Musso, the escapee from Huntsville, showing his face near or around Victoria Lucas at her warehouse?"

The captain, with an uninterested tone, commented back, "Well, Agent Tillman, we have been busy catching all our local drug dealers and really haven't had time to investigate the FBI's list!"

Rod, realizing the captain's negative vocalizing, interjected, "I thought we were all on the same team, Captain."

The captain looked up from his desk and sarcastically questioned, "And what team is that, Agent Tillman?"

Rod, painfully aware that he was not going to get much help from the Laredo Police Department, slowly turned away and commented, in an effort to make a point, "I guess we will just have to flood Laredo with more FBI agents to catch our drug dealers!" Rod then continued out the front door, heading to the McClelland Street warehouse, still with a very precautionary posture, expecting followers to make an effort to locate Katrina, as he opened the door of his black sedan.

CHAPTER 26
THE PARACHUTE

Nicholas, standing near the two planes, could not help but notice that one plane was first loaded and about only a third of the packages remained to be loaded on the second plane, the one in which he was the passenger. He also took note, as he observed the packages, that the ones being loaded on his plane had a small orange dot sticker on each. Once all was loaded, his pilot approached him and questioned, "You ready to go, Señor?"

With now a very suspicious look, Nicholas replied, "Yeah, let's get going, AMIGO!" The pilot opened the cockpit door and pulled out what appeared to be a backpack. Nicholas walked around the back end of the plane, and as he did, he looked closer and distinguished that it was not a backpack but a parachute. He then began to contemplate that his plane was the obvious decoy. Nicholas next climbed into the plane and speculated about why Victoria would not just shoot him at the warehouse if she wanted him dead. He then concluded she wanted a body in the crashed decoy. The pilot revved up the engine as they watched the other plane lift up and angle upward to the right. Again rethinking the scenario, Nicholas squinted his eyes and told himself, "Two birds with one stone!" He then mumbled in an extremely under-his-breath tone, "She needs a body, she will get a body."

THE PARACHUTE

—⚡︎—

Rod drove up to the warehouse on McClelland. He exited his vehicle and knocked on the single-door entry facing the street. One of Victoria's Latino henchmen answered the door with "May I help you, Señor?"

Rod looked straight at him and asked, "Is Ms. Victoria Lucas in?"

The Latino then questioned, "And who can I say is calling?"

Rod now glanced to the right and back as he flashed his badge and credentials. "Yes, I am Rod Tillman of the FBI, and she knows me well."

The Latino then answered, "One moment, Señor," and closed the door. Next, Victoria appeared at the door in a white pants ensemble with a gold chain and a large pendant and matching hoop earrings, her brown eyes glistening in the sunlight peering through the open door as she inquired "To what do I owe the pleasure of this visit, Officer Tillman?" She then sarcastically remarked, "I have not shot or assaulted Katrina, as you have continued to imply as my sole purpose in life!"

Rod then remarked, with a half grin, "And I appreciate your cooperation in that matter, but that is not why I am here."

Victoria then, in a curious vein, asked, "So why are you here?"

Rod then explained, "I am looking for the whereabouts of one Mr. Nicholas Musso, an escaped convict from the Huntsville prison."

Victoria then, in a matter-of-fact statement, replied, "And why would I know the whereabouts of Mr. Nicholas Musso?"

Rod, now enjoying the banter, emphatically implicated her: "Because we all know that your father broke him out of Huntsville detention and included him in the transport of illegal drugs into this country!"

Victoria, now in an angry but cautious demeanor, replied, "Prove it!" as she slammed the door shut in Rod's face. Rod shook his head and turned back toward his vehicle and headed across the street.

—⁂—

Nicholas was now glaring out the cockpit window, looking down at the landscape over Mexico as they were nearing Nuevo Laredo, Mexico, just south of the border of Laredo, Texas. He knew that it would not be long before the pilot would bail. He observed a short wooden club on the pilot's left, which he watched out of the corner of his eye as the Latino pilot slowly slipped his hand to grip it. Nicholas then noticed a large open prairie with few trees and decided this was where it was coming, and with a lift of his left elbow, in a surprise to the pilot, he swung with all his force and in one motion clipped him straight under his nose. The pilot went completely unconscious, falling forward onto the plane's controls, as Nicholas struggled to pull up the parachute. Nicholas placed his arms into the shoulder straps and searched for the pull lever to release the chute for opening. He knew time was short, as the plane now began a downward spiral. Nicholas opened the cockpit door on his right and forced his way out and pulled the chute's release in a sequence motion as he exited the plane. The chute opened immediately as he glided toward the earth. The plane could be seen crashing into a bordering wooded area outside Nuevo Laredo, and the flames shot up in the air from the impact.

—⁂—

The cargo-carrying plane arrived back at the secluded airport. Victoria was standing adjacent to the hanger while the Cessna

THE PARACHUTE

taxied up. The pilot from the loaded plane exited and walked up to Victoria, and she, in a very controlled voice, asked, "Everything went as planned?"

The pilot shook his head and responded, "*Si*, Señorita, all went as planned!"

Victoria, still wishing for assurance, again demanded, "You saw the other plane go down?"

The pilot then, in a convincing manner, said, "*Si*, Señorita, I saw the flames before we landed."

Victoria was feeling a moment of confidence when her cell phone rang. She pulled the phone from her pocket and glanced at the caller. "Nicholas!" She answered and said, "Hello?"

The voice on the other end, in a low, demonic tone, stated, "Well, now we know who the real traitor is! You have your body!"

Nicholas, lying on the ground with a busted ankle, snapped his phone closed. The Mexican *policia*, with blaring lights and sirens, headed toward the crash site as Nicholas watched, now sitting up. He was now trying to decide, with his incapacitated body, whether he wanted the attention of the police or not. The situation would arouse suspicions with his parachute, the plane crash, and alerts from the FBI after his escape from prison. "The other elephant in the room" was his possibly being attacked by prairie wolves after dark. He crawled around until he found a branch from a prairie brush he could use as a crutch. He remained inconspicuous as he began to hobble toward the city lights.

—⋙—

Victoria was now deeply troubled over the same concern as Rod Tillman, that being the whereabouts of Nicholas Musso, the only difference being she was worried about her own personal well-being. She drove back to the warehouse, and as she approached, she noticed a strange black sedan parked out front. She got out of her vehicle and walked up to the entrance and opened the door to view Ramon Costello, along with three of his goons, sitting at a table in the open area of the shop, sitting back from the foyer. Victoria, not cognizant of Mr. Costello's appearance, in a very suspicious manner questioned, "And you are?"

Costello, politely and in an amused response, said, "Why, hello, Ms. Lucas. I am Ramon Costello."

Victoria, being already upset about the existence of Nicholas, tilted her head to the right and inquisitively questioned, "Nice to meet you—and you are here all the way from California because?"

Costello smiled and explained, "I am here, Ms. Lucas, looking for Mr. Nicholas Musso!"

Victoria immediately retorted, "Well, if he ain't the man of the hour!" She then added, "Mr. Costello, to tell you the truth, I just tried to blow him up in Mexico, and the son of a bitch is still alive!"

Costello then presented her with "You see, Ms. Lucas, someone owes me money and has to account for the loss of two of my best men."

Victoria then burst out in a humorous voice, "Mr. Costello, I will tell you where he is, and you can do me a favor and take him out."

Costello, not seemingly satisfied with the resolve of Victoria, provided an ultimatum with "No, Ms. Lucas, I don't think you understand the circumstances you are faced with. You must be responsible for your men and pay for the consequences of their actions!"

Victoria, now feeling attacked with the fact that this head of a Cartel had come from California and was seriously pissed over the loss of his men, which had now placed her in a whole new corner,

THE PARACHUTE

decided she was left with no alternatives. She reached into one of her Latinos' pockets and pulled out a 9-millimeter and aimed directly at Mr. Costello's head and pulled the trigger, striking him directly in the forehead. She then shot one of his henchmen in the chest while the other two were struggling to pull their weapons. Two of her Latinos drew their weapons and shot each of the remaining henchmen. Victoria then, with a desperate look on her face, exclaimed, "I have no fucking idea what I just did and what the consequences of this will bring, but I'd had enough threats for one day!" She then mandated to her Latino crew, "Remove these bodies, and they are never to be found, *comprende?*" The Latinos scurried to haul the dead bodies away.

The night sounds surrounded Nicholas as he continued to limp with his makeshift crutch toward a metal building behind a local residence on the edge of the city of Nuevo Laredo. A young boy of about six years old in a dirty T-shirt, shorts, and sandals ran up to him, questioning him in Spanish, "Señor are you hurt?"

Nicholas, somewhat comprehending the boy's concern, replied, "*Si*, mama, poppa?"

The boy, understanding Nicholas, turned and ran to the house yelling, "Mama, Mama." The mother, hearing her son, immediately responded, but when she saw Nicholas she retreated in fear of him harming her and the boy. Upon noticing he was injured, she hesitantly approached and, in broken English, asked, "Señor, you broke your leg?" Nicholas then, exhausted, fell to the ground and passed out.

The table at Katrina's new residence was set as the doorbell rang and Rod patiently awaited.

Katrina opened the door and again, maintaining her hidden identity, stood back. Rod walked in, and she grabbed his hands. Rod's shy indifference was apparent, as usual, as he reassured her that Victoria was presently not interested in her location. Katrina then questioned, "Am I finally getting to a court date?"

Rod then, in a positive motion, related, "I think we are close for a hearing, but I am trying to locate all the culprits involved in that whole setup." Rod then quizzed, Katrina, "Do you remember any of the people Gus Lucas had as close associates while he was importing drugs?"

Katrina then took a deep breath and, in a weak reply, stated, "Rod, I was poor and needed money and did whatever they told me to do!" She then finished with "I know you think I am a whore and very stupid, but I was not allowed to be involved with the big shots in their business."

Rod then quickly answered, "No, Katrina, I do not think you are a whore, and you certainly are not stupid, but you must remember a couple of key personnel of Gus Lucas." Katrina, somewhat in fear, looked down, and Rod retorted, "Let's eat."

Nicholas woke up facing the young boy that had first greeted him when he arrived in the dark of night, along with two other children, all staring at him, the oddity in the room. In a moment, the mother walked in dressed in a plain and simple sackcloth-type dress and sandals, her hair pulled into a knotted ponytail. She was approximately 5 foot 4 inches tall and about thirty-five years old and had a perfect olive complexion and soft, large brown eyes. She scurried the

THE PARACHUTE

children out of the room and pointed to his bandaged and wrapped left ankle. She remarked, "It is not broke, but you no walk, Señor."

Nicholas was now feeling some relief from the security of being inside and even being ministered to, but the pain in his leg was extremely irritating. He observed that there was no male head of the household milling around. He questioned the young woman by first asking her name: "*Nombre?*"

She smiled and immediately responded, "Isabella." She pointed to him in a gesture of questioning his name.

Nicholas responded, "John," and then, realizing he needed to put a Spanish touch on the subject, "Juan." Nicholas then asked, "Where husband?" and again, with the little Spanish he had picked up, "*Donde* Poppa?"

Isabella then answered, with a wave of her hand, "Poppa work, but will come home!" The indication brought a sincere concern to Nicholas, as he then attempted to retreat from the wood-frame bed, but then he fell back, as the pain was excruciating.

Isabella quickly grabbed his shoulder and remarked, "Señor, you no go." She pointed again to his leg. "*No muy bien.*" With her broken English, she again exclaimed, "Not very good." Nicholas was defenseless in his condition. He remembered that before he had departed from Laredo, he had stuffed five hundred-dollar bills in his pocket, which he originally hid in his boot before Felipo kidnapped him. He reached in his pocket and handed two of the hundred-dollar bills to Isabella, and she, with a surprised look, questioned his generosity but stated, "You no pay, Señor." Nicholas instantly knew this was a good, honest woman and insisted she take the money. She smiled again and held the money against her breast as if to say he was the answer to her prayers.

CHAPTER 27
BETH MAKES IT

Rod, sitting in his vehicle with the Laredo Police Department in the background, contemplating the status of Nicholas's whereabouts, pulled out his cell phone. He called Brad and expressed his thoughts: "Brad, I've been thinking, and I don't think that woman back at that cabin in California told me the whole story!" Rod continued, "She saw more than she is telling me."

Brad responded, with a slight drag and groan, "Well, Rod, maybe you left there too quick, 'cause she went home and is back in Oregon."

Rod then, with an investigative lure to bring Brad in line with his thinking, inquired, "Can we put a twenty-four-hour surveillance on her in Oregon and see what she is up to?"

Brad then questioned Rod, "What are we looking for, Rod?"

Rod then explained, "I think there is something more to her and Nicholas." Rod then finished with "Who knows—Nicholas may show up there!"

Beth was sitting in front of her vanity as her cell phone rang, and she answered with "Hello."

The voice of Nicholas put a smile on her face as he responded with "Beth?"

Beth then questioned, "Where are you? How are you?"

Nicholas then in a calm voice again answered, "I am OK, and I am in Mexico."

Beth then reacted, "Where in Mexico?"

Nicholas defined, "Look, I am in Nuevo Laredo, near the Texas border, but I need you to listen." He then explained, "I need you to get the money and use whatever you need to fly to Laredo, Texas, rent a car and cross the border, and come to Nuevo Laredo and meet me!"

Beth then stuttered for a moment and asked, "When do I leave?"

Nicholas then again told her, "Tomorrow. Close up your house for a month, and come meet me."

Beth, now beaming with joy, in an excited tone told Nicholas, "I will leave tomorrow, and can I call when I get to Laredo?"

Nicholas then interjected, "Yes, all is safe! Call me when you get to the airport and rent a car, and just come!"

The same judge as previously ruled on the case, now leaning over, having a conversation with the assistant DA and Katrina's court-appointed attorney, shook his head in agreement. Katrina and Rod sat quietly at the defense table, awaiting the judge's ruling on Katrina's fate. The attorneys each returned to their respective seats, with Katrina's attorney explaining, as he sat, the judge's tentative thoughts. Katrina looked up and immediately questioned in a hopeless tone, "Am I going to jail?"

The attorney raised his hand in a calming motion and explained, "Hold on, Katrina. I don't think that is where the judge is going with this, but in any case, he is not going to make that decision today."

In that moment, the judge hit his gavel and exclaimed in an elevated voice, "In the district attorney's case 19669 against Katrina Martinez, a noncitizen of the United States, for the deadly assault on Mr. Gustave Lucas, I will render my judgement in three days." The judge then ruled, "Ms. Katrina Martinez will remain in the restricted custody of the FBI for appearance in this court at 10:00 a.m. Thursday, August 3."

Miguel Costello, son of Ramon Costello, now reviewing his father's carefully planned logbook as outlined in a day-by-day calendar, saw Victoria Lucas's name and phone number. He then noticed that his father and three of their best soldiers had flown out to see Ms. Lucas five days ago, and he had not heard from him. Miguel tried to call his father for the third time and got no answer. He now dialed Victoria's cell, and she noticed the area code for California and decided not to answer. Miguel left a message: "Ms. Lucas, this is Miguel Costello, son of Ramon Costello, and my father flew out to meet you, and I have not been able to reach him." Miguel then ended with "Would you be so kind as to return my call or have my father give me a call?" Victoria listened to the message and pondered what she should do. She thought that responding that she never saw him might be the best deterrent to keep the wolves away.

BETH MAKES IT

Beth was now at the Portland airport, sitting at the gate, waiting for a flight to Houston and then connecting for a short leg to Laredo. Almost simultaneously an undercover agent was pulling up to her home in Oregon. Beth, cautiously keeping her hand on the black bag on the adjacent seat next to her containing all the cash, awaited the boarding call. This was a definite carry-on. She had purchased a first-class ticket to keep all her personal items close and secure. She boarded the plane, placed the bag in the overhead compartment, and sat directly beneath the enclosure. She pulled out her cell phone and dialed Nicholas's number. Nicholas, seeing the call was from her, immediately answered, "Yes!"

Beth, excited, responded quickly, "I am on the plane, and I have the cargo."

He efficiently retorted, "Good, can't wait to see you. Rent a car and call me again." He then hung up. Nicholas had now relocated to a local Mexican motel to await Beth's arrival and remain somewhat hidden from Victoria's possible tracking of his location.

Two days had passed, and Miguel Costello became concerned about his father's disappearance and now, hearing no response from Victoria, decided to pay a visit to Victoria. He called his father's private flight service and signaled his Latin guard to get four more guys for a trip. Miguel was now pulling up in two black SUVs to a secluded airport in Southern California, where he and five of his guys boarded his father's private jet. Once he was seated on the plane, a private attendant wearing a short skirt and open blouse and a colorful scarf around her neck placed a cocktail on the side table. Miguel pulled out his cell phone and again pulled up Victoria's number and called. This time Victoria answered with a tone of uncertainty to throw off Miguel. "Hello?"

Miguel responded immediately, "Ms. Lucas, how are you?"

She then questioned, "Who is this?"

Miguel explained, "I am Miguel Costello, son of Ramon Costello, and I am trying to contact him." Miguel proceeded further, "He had you on his logbook a week ago, and we have not heard back from him since."

Victoria, searching her thoughts for the best escape, took a breath and insinuated, in her usual performance, "Your father did call, Mr. Costello, and he did indicate he was coming to see me, but I have not heard from him since."

Miguel realized this was all a lie because he knew his father was insistent in making the Lucas cartel responsible for his losses and would not have let them off the hook so easy. Miguel then looked at the pilot and signaled with a hand gesture to take off. Victoria held the phone to her chin and worried he will come looking eventually.

—⁂—

Beth arrived in Laredo and rented a car and then called Nicholas again: "I am here!"

Nicholas expressed, "Whoa, I am anxious to see you!" He then explained, "Follow your map and cross the border into Nuevo Laredo." Nicholas then provided her with directions to his location, which was a discreet hacienda and border housing to maintain his anonymity.

Beth continued, as she was so excited about the rendezvous, "I was so nervous when that FBI guy approached me!"

Nicholas then questioned, "You don't think they followed you?"

Beth immediately responded, "No, I don't think so, because I left the park and went home and you called." She then added, "I left the next day, and I don't think they would have set up that quick."

Nicholas, somewhat questioning the reality, then reaffirmed, "I agree, because he had just discovered your existence that day." He finished with "We are OK—please get here."

Beth softly whispered, "I love you!"

CHAPTER 28
WHERE'S MY FATHER?

Rod and Katrina were in each other's embrace on the edge of the bed in her secluded residence amid the suburban area of Laredo. Rod, in a calm voice, confirmed to Katrina, "Tomorrow morning, we go back to court for the judge's final judgment."

Katrina nervously responded, "Suppose he sends me back to jail?" and she continued, in a moan, "Rod, I can't go back to jail."

Rod reassured her, "Look—if he intended to incarcerate you permanently, he would not have let you out on bail under our custody." Rod then finished with "He will probably place you in a halfway house with community service, but you are not going to prison."

Katrina, her arms tightly around Rod, murmured out "You better be right, because I need you close!" as she then pulled his face close, and together they rolled over in the bed.

Miguel Costello and his cartel associates deplaned at the municipal airport wearing black suits, hair slicked back, with serious beady eyes as again two black SUVs with drivers were driven up to their position on the runway. The drivers were obvious rental agents being paid to deliver the vehicles. One of the Costello henchmen handed each of the drivers an envelope with a tip, and he slid into shotgun position in the front seat. Miguel got into the rear of one of the SUVs with two other of his associates, while the two remaining heavy physiques, dark-haired, well-dressed, obvious gunmen, quickly got into the other SUV. They drove out of the airport, headed to the metropolis of Laredo. Miguel questioned, "Do we have an address?"

The front-seat henchman replied, "*Si*, Señor Miguel, I got the address from Mr. Ramon's secretary, Cecilia."

The night passed, and as early morning with an overcast and a slight drizzle of rain began, Rod and Katrina sat at the kitchen table staring at each other for a moment. Rod stood and hugged Katrina and then whispered in her ear, "It will be OK!" They exited the kitchen door and both got into Rod's sedan. Rod surveyed the vicinity around the house before pulling out, as he still did not trust Victoria. He put the vehicle in reverse and backed out of the driveway and told Katrina, "Just for precaution, would you mind putting your head down until we pull out of here?" Katrina, now with a fearful look, slowly slipped down in the passenger seat as Rod accelerated quickly down the street. He then instructed her, "It is OK now, but when we get to the courthouse, let me exit first, and I will have two agents there to escort you into the courthouse."

Katrina, very anxious, questioned, "Do you think that they are still trying to kill me?"

Rod immediately interjected, "No, but I am always being cautious until this is over and you are out of here!"

Katrina then, with a look of suspicion, inquired, "Am I leaving, Rod?"

Rod turned and gave Katrina an impatient look and questioned, "Katrina, you don't want to stay in this city with this Gus Lucas cartel threatening your life daily, do you?"

—⁂—

Miguel, with the address of Victoria's warehouse, used the GPS to direct him and his crew to the location. The lead associate sitting to his right in the rear of the SUV questioned Miguel, "Do you have a plan, Miguel?"

Miguel replied, "Well, that depends on Ms. Victoria Lucas and the whereabouts of my father and his health."

The side associate again questioned, "So we may have to force it out of her?" The associate continually professed, "She will have men with guns also, *amigo*!"

Miguel interjected in a sleazy voice, "We have the element of surprise, and we will hold our position very carefully until the moment is right!" He then mandated, "I expect all of you to pay attention and be ready." He then raised his eyebrow and asked, "*Comprende?*"

—⁂—

Rod and Katrina now pulled up to the courthouse, and as Rod had planned, two agents in flannel suits awaited their arrival. One of the agents opened the door for Katrina, and she exited as Rod got out and immediately swept around the front of the vehicle to escort her himself. Rod surveyed the surroundings as he and Katrina walked through the front door of the courthouse. Everyone sitting about in open areas and hallways looked suspicious, and Rod, now being extra cautious, remembered the unexpected events that seemed to have plagued him and Katrina. After going through security, Rod and Katrina took the elevator to the third floor and entered the courtroom. Katrina's case, being first on the docket, sent them immediately to the front of the courtroom. Katrina continued to the table where her attorney awaited, while Rod took a seat along the bench behind the rail and Katrina's chair.

Miguel's two SUVs pulled up along Victoria's warehouse and then circled the block to investigate and survey the surroundings for possible impending sabotage. The vehicles, after a second round, pulled up and stopped down the street in the next block, in front of another abandoned warehouse adjacent to an open lot. Both vehicles drove onto the open lot, and all six men jumped out and retrieved rifles and automatic weapons, along with a missile launcher, from the rear of the vehicles. The drivers remained in each of the black units as four of Miguel's men moved up the block toward Victoria's warehouse to get in position. Miguel and his key associate walked toward the warehouse's front door. The associate knocked on the door, and one of Victoria's henchmen answered and questioned, "Can I help you, Señor?"

The associate informed him, "Yes, we are here to see Ms. Victoria Lucas."

The henchman then asked, "Do you have an appointment?"

Miguel then spoke up: "Tell Ms. Lucas that Miguel Costello from California would like to speak with her."

The henchman responded, "Wait here, and I will see if she is here!" The henchman closed the door and disappeared to the back. Miguel, with a worried look on his face, turned to check on his defense's locations.

THE RESOLVE

The judge called Katrina's case to order, and the bailiff read the docket number. The judge began to pontificate on Katrina's case and present status. "Miss Martinez, you have been charged with second-degree murder of a man who was already in custody and defenseless against any such aggression. He was dependent on his safety, being handcuffed by the Laredo Police Department, and you took advantage of this position and shot and killed this man." The judge continued, "Although this man was a noted murderer, cartel leader, and racketeer who was wanted by the FBI for the listed charges and who has now also been linked to the attempts on your life, we cannot condone or be an enabler, in our system of justice, of such unlawful activity." The judge then concluded with "I have given deep consideration to this case, looked at all the evidence, and studied the attacks on you, which included much suffering and almost took your life. I have come to a decision, which is as follows: I am sentencing you to five years in prison, suspended with a court order that your current visa is canceled and you return to your own country and not be allowed back into the United States of America for a period of five years." The judge then added, "The court understands your agony, Miss Martinez, and your own attempt of defense against such a lawless man; however, we have laws that we must adhere to in this country." The judge then slammed the gavel down and finished with "This case is closed!"

Miguel and his associates, after waiting and seeing no return of Victoria's henchman, opened the door and walked into the entrance of the warehouse. They stood looking at the inventory and around

WHERE'S MY FATHER?

the room. Victoria and two of her armed men entered, and she, in a sarcastic innuendo, questioned, "See anything you like, Mr. Costello?" She was now standing across the floor in the warehouse in a long black skirt, and her red lips and her long black hair combed straight to her shoulders almost gave her the appearance of the cartoon witch in *Snow White*. Her two armed guards stood like sentries, ready for a confrontation.

Miguel responded, with a cautious tone in his voice, "Hello, Ms. Lucas. You know why we are here, as my father came to visit you and has never been heard from since."

Victoria, now realizing the quagmire she had now created for herself, attempted to placate Miguel as she created a scenario for a possible resolution. She stepped forward and looked Miguel straight in the eyes and in a convincing voice said, "Miguel, your father did come, and we sat at that table, and I explained to him that the loss of my father, the bombing of our warehouse in Colombia, and now the confiscation of all our product by Mr. Musso had left us in a financial crisis. He spent the night, we drank, we slept, and he vowed to honor the code of the cartels."

Miguel, with suspicion and doubt dominating his thoughts, immediately questioned, "Very creative of you, Ms. Lucas, but where is he now?" Victoria, now already deep in the pool of the lie, carried it all the way and responded, "You see, Miguel, your father and I fell in love, and he said he would go to Colombia and secure the remaining supply for us both." She continued, "He did not want to tell you because of our relationship, at least not now!"

Miguel then stared at Victoria and, in a frustrated tone, threw his hands in the air and exclaimed as he walked out, "I will get to the bottom of this!"

THE RESOLVE

Embracing each other, Rod and Katrina were back at the rented house as Rod, with a relieved but sympathetic expression, told Katrina, "Look, if you come back and settle in Nuevo Laredo, Mexico, just across the border, we could see each other often!" This was not exactly what Katrina wanted to hear at the moment. Rod, in an effort to upscale the mood, explained, "Look, Katrina, you are so lucky you were not incarcerated, and this afforded freedom left a door for us to see each other!"

Katrina, in a bittersweet tone, but hoping for more from Rod, replied, "Yes, Rod and I am so appreciative of all you've done, and I know I am so fortunate to be free, but I love you, and I want to be near you all the time. I can't be alone in Mexico and not be able to see you and touch you!"

Rod, in an exasperated but controlled voice, resolved with "Katrina, I have those feelings for you, but I can't be an FBI man in Mexico, at least not now. We have to settle for the moment for what we have." Rod finished with "We need a vacation. How about a week in Cozumel?"

Katrina, now realizing she had placed Rod in a very difficult position with her demands and his job, decided to accept his proposal. She again embraced him and stared into his eyes and admitted, "You are right, and I should be very appreciative of what you are trying to do." She then concluded with "I would love to go to Cozumel with you, and then I will go visit my family." Rod, with a sigh of relief, with a half grin, expressed, "This is the best we can do for now, Katrina."

CHAPTER 29
MIGUEL'S PLAN

Beth and Nicholas, in an embrace, were kissing as they leaned against the vehicle Beth had rented in Laredo, Texas. Nicholas stared into her eyes and asked, "Are you ready to get out of here?"

Beth answered in an anxious tone, "Yes, I missed you, and I thought you were gone forever."

Nicholas, in his low, gravelly tone, interjected, "We have to head south for a while! How much time do you have?"

Beth, with her eyes glowing in anticipation, again responded, "I locked my house up for a month, and I have the car for whatever." Nicholas then, with a direct look, explained, "You realize now what we are dealing with, and they know I am not dead, but Victoria Lucas thinks I am out for revenge and is waiting for me!" Nicholas then, in a sarcastic expression, finished with "But I am not going after her and going to disappear, and that will drive her crazy!"

Beth, not concerned, questioned, "Nicholas, what happens down the road? Will you go back for revenge?" She then pleaded, "We don't need any money with what you have here and what I have—we can live comfortably!"

Nicholas then, in a decisive voice, stated, "Let's take one step at a time, but for now we need to get out of here!" They both got into the car and drove off.

—⚞—

The black SUV was still parked. Miguel, staring at the warehouse, instructed the driver to pull out. He turned to his associate henchman and, in a frustrated manner and pointing his finger at the warehouse as they pull out, he said, "She knows where my father is, and she is lying to us!" He then turned his head and faced the front as he completed his assertion in an aggressive vocalization: "She will pay for this lie and tell me where my father is now and wish she had never lied!" Miguel then told the driver to find the nearest hotel that would provide them with the needed obscurity they, for now, wished to maintain.

The associate commented to Miguel, "The more hotels and people around, the less the authorities will notice us, Señor."

Miguel again turned and looked at his associate and, with a chuckle, asked, "And you thought of that all by yourself?"

—⚞—

Brad Kingsworth and Rod were now sitting across the table from each other back in the Houston office as Brad questioned Rod, "Has Katrina packed up and left the country?"

Rod then opened up to Brad: "Yeah, the judge gave her a week to pack up and leave the country with a patrol unit escorting her to the border." Rod continued with "I am going to miss her."

Brad sympathetically responded, "I kinda knew the two of you had a thing for each other." Then Brad, in a jovial conjecture, added,

MIGUEL'S PLAN

"I mean, what man would not fall head over heels for a woman who first tried to electrocute him and then left him for dead?"

Rod sat back and folded his arms and, with a half grin, cynically retorted, "Well, Brad, I can see that romantic pile of emotions you have been holding back has finally been released!"

Miguel and his henchmen were sitting around the hotel pool in the bright sun, looking very much out of place in their dark suits surrounded by all the sunbathers, as they contemplated their next move. Miguel was now telling his chief associate, "We need to get Ms. Victoria in a secure location so that we can press the truth from that lying *chiquita*."

His associate replied, "Señor Miguel, this is her town, not ours! We need a plan!"

Miguel then questioned, "What do you suggest, *mi amigo*?"

The associate then replied, "We use force at night when they are asleep and show her we mean business!" He then continued, "This is the way your poppa Ramon would do this!"

Miguel was not yet convinced that a show of force would bring about the result he wanted as he touched his lips with his forefinger. He expressed his thoughts aloud: "If my father has been murdered by this bitch, then we want all her product, and blowing up everything may remove that opportunity and invite the feds."

Busy packing her things for the move back to Mexico, Katrina heard a knock and was startled.

She first thought it was Rod and ran to the front door but remembered Rod had a key. He would not knock. She peered through a side curtain and saw a tall man in a black suit with no tie. She thought it might be an agent coming to check on her and discuss her departure. However, the open collar and no tie waved a red flag in her mind. She questioned, "Who is it?"

The man answered, "I am with customs, here to check your passport?"

Katrina, panicking, replied, "I need a moment." She ran back to the bedroom and phoned Rod. Rod answered, "Hey, you OK?"

Katrina's voice was trembling, but she clearly blurted out, "There is a man outside my door telling me he is with customs and he needs to check my passport!"

Rod, now raising his voice, exclaimed, "Do not let him in. I am in Houston and on my way, but I can have two patrol units over there in minutes. Stall him!"

Katrina clicked off her phone and in the same moment heard the front door kicked in and the voice of the man, very low and gravelly, explaining, "Katrina, you know you have to pay for Gus Lucas, the man you murdered, and now you are walking free!"

Katrina, panicking, further rushed into the bedroom, locked the door, and attempted to climb out the window as the bedroom door was kicked in and the man fired two shots. The first shot pierced the wall next to the window, and the next shattered the glass as Katrina fell to the ground, scrabbled to pull herself up, and ran toward the street. The shooter approached the window and saw Katrina running away. He then turned and headed to the front door, and as he exited out to the front porch, two Laredo patrol units pulled up in front with lights flashing. One of the officers, observing the shooter exiting the house with the gun, attempted to engage him, aiming his gun. The shooter pointed, aimed, and shot the officer in the chest. Rounds were fired from the second unit, striking the assailant in the head and shoulder. The assailant dropped immediately to the ground. Katrina ran to the officer of the second unit, who was now approaching the wounded officer to assist him. Katrina screamed, "Is he dead?"

The officer, now kneeling to attend to his fellow patrolman, looked up at Katrina and stated, "I think he will be OK. That other guy is dead for sure!"

Miguel instructed his chieftain to check out a motel on the outskirts of Laredo for them to abduct Victoria to and be secluded. Miguel further said, "An old warehouse away from her place would be even better, but the rental may be too obvious." He then told his associate, "We also need more weapons in case our quiet night attack is not so quiet."

The associate then shook his head in agreement and murmured, "*Si*, Señor, I get your point."

Miguel then quietly reiterated the serious need to remain quiet and then informed him, "Check back in California with my cousin Felix Costello and see if he has any connection in this area where we may find some firepower." Miguel then leaned back in the chaise recliner by the pool and puffed on a half-remaining cigar.

Katrina, now sitting back in the Laredo Police Department rear interrogation room, was sobbing with a white tissue up to her nose.

THE RESOLVE

Rod walked in, and she jumped up, and he embraced her in his arms and expressed, "Thank God you are OK."

Katrina, exhausted from all the trauma, in an exasperated tone responded, "Rod, never leave me here alone again!" and finished with "I can't take this anymore!"

Rod, realizing her present condition, first tried to calm her down and reassure her this would never happen again as he added, "Katrina, I totally understand how you feel, and you will be with me until we can get you out of here."

Katrina then, in a moment of logic, questioned, "How did they find the house, and if they can find that, what stops them from finding me at my house in Mexico?"

Rod, very aware of the insecurity she justifiably had laid out, now attempted to plan her departure but first asked, "Who besides you has ever discussed the location of your family?"

Katrina, in an impish mannerism, said, "No one that I can remember, but you will come and stay with me at first until I feel safe, won't you?"

Rod then, as he looked up at the ceiling, followed with "Yes, but if anyone tracks my whereabouts in the FBI web, they can locate me!" He then, in a calculating and controlled expression, explained, "We need to meet in another location separate and away from your family."

Katrina, standing back and staring at him, no longer with the insecure, sheepish voice, frantically stated, "I will never be safe, Rod!" She then questioned, "If they can follow you, hell, they can follow me!"

Rod, again comprehending her fear, replied, "Not if we totally erase you from our computers!" He then ended with "That will take some doing, but I think I can convince them to get it done for your safety."

Katrina looked down at the floor and, in a sad display, emphasized her endless predicament again as she said, "I feel doomed, Rod, and you will never be assured of my complete safety!"

Rod, now taking a different approach in an effort to provide a source of strength, responded, "Katrina, you are tougher than this. You knew there were risks involved when you hooked up with Lucas and his gang!"

Katrina, immediately insulted, expressed, "Watch your words, FBI man!"

Rod, shaking his head with a half chuckle, answered, "I am sorry, and I hear you, but I kept you mostly safe this long, and you will just have to trust that I have the balls and brains to protect you!"

Katrina smiled and threw her arms around him.

Brad, after hearing about another attack on Katrina, called Rod and inquired, "Is she OK, Rod?"

Rod responded, "Yeah, but Brad, these continual attempts on her life are draining her, and I got to tell you, me too!"

Brad then replied, "We got to get her out of here and to a place they can't find her and she is safe."

Rod then countered with "Look, Brad, I need a vacation, and I am planning to take her with me!"

Brad, with his unique sense of humor, laughed and mumbled out, "What a service we in the FBI provide." Then he, in a supportive voice, added, "You deserve a vacation, Rod, so go and enjoy!" Brad shook his head and again stated under his breath, "I can't believe I just said that."

CHAPTER 30
THE VACATION

The two SUVs parked, at 1:22 a.m., a block down from Victoria's warehouse in the glimmer of streetlights as night insects were whirling around to the attraction of the illumination above. Miguel Costello stared straight ahead and saw no movement on the street and, in a low tone, instructed his main associate to take three others and use a crowbar to pry open the door with minimal noise. He further directed, "Ms. Lucas's room is across the warehouse floor. Cover her mouth with the wet chloroform and carry her out unharmed." Miguel then finished with "Remember, she may be my father's *puta*" as they both chuckled.

The associate, in a distinguishable but half-mixed Spanish accent questioned, "Señor Miguel, surely this *puta* will have alarms?"

Miguel answered, "Of course she may have alarms—that is why we have the big guns in the trunk! We discussed this!"

The associate again questioned, "But Señor, we may shoot Ms. Lucas!"

Miguel immediately, in a loud voice, responded, "Then don't return, because I am going to blow your head off, you idiot! This was our whole mission, you dumbass!" Miguel then continued to expound his point anxiously: "Have you not been listening? I have to get her alone to find my father!" The associate jumped out of the vehicle, and he walked toward the SUV directly behind him as the three other henchmen exited the vehicle, and he explained in Spanish and broken English while they all extracted the automatic weapons from the rear of the SUV. One of the men, in an anxious rush, dropped one of the automatic weapons behind the vehicle. Miguel, focusing on his plan and already having doubts with this crew, took a deep breath and shook his head.

Victoria's eyes were awake and glistening from the reflection from the light in another room as she lay quietly in the massive king-size bed. She was listening to every creak in the building in a worried anticipation of Miguel's return. She heard off-and-on street traffic, but very infrequently, being situated in a warehouse district at approximately two in the morning. Then the sound of voices mumbling in Spanish were apparent, as if explaining how to do something or giving direction. Victoria, now fully awake, continued to hear the words even though not understanding the conversation of the individuals. The obvious clank of metal against metal prompted her to immediately sit up, as the sounds were now more pronounced. She slipped out of bed and departed from her bedroom door and headed to a window in the warehouse facing the street. She saw the shadows of the men and their movement surrounding the front door. She returned immediately back into her room and grabbed a 9-millimeter from her dresser drawer and then rushed to her new chieftain, David Valdez, and opened his door and in the lowest but clearest vocal plea for help said, "Daveed! Wake up! They are here!"

David, immediately comprehending Victoria's excitement, sprang from his cot and quietly exited to collect the other men. The main door in the warehouse was finally pushed open, but not without an alarming bang. David and his men retrieved their automatic weapons from an adjacent storage closet in a corridor of the warehouse and set up at all the doorways that opened to the main room. Just as Miguel's men entered the front entry, a round of automatic gunfire hit two of them, and they all retreated back through the exit. Miguel, leaning against the exterior wall and observing the failed plan, screamed, "You bastards, you made too much noise and woke them all!" He angrily continued with a high, shrill voice, "Take cover and shoot the windows! We will take them out!" The gunfire continued as bullets flew, ricocheting off the interior walls and furniture. Victoria's men were now huddling behind tables in the large room amid the smoke-filled air, splintering wood fragments, and wall penetrations, with the floor now covered in shell casings.

Sirens from a distance could be heard, alerting Miguel that time was short as he motioned his finger back to the parked vehicles and demanded of his head guy, "Get the missile launcher, now!" and blurted out, "We will kill them all!" His lead henchman ran to the vehicle and opened the rear lift gate while he noticed the drivers exiting the two SUVs and running down the street. He fired his weapon in their direction but missed them completely. He grabbed the plastic tube with a strap hanging, the army-issue military missile launcher. He turned and headed back to the blazing, violent environment coming from the warehouse. Miguel pulled the tube from his man's hands, snapped open the plastic cover, and took a stance, aligning himself with the front door. The moment prior to his firing the missile, a bullet clipped him in the shoulder, causing him to fall backward and forcing his shot to penetrate an upper window, which obliterated the second-story interior. The futile attempt angered Miguel. His men were now looking at one another as they all realized the conditions and the failing, futile attempt. They were outnumbered, and now two of their men were down. They continued looking at Miguel, waiting for a white flag of surrendering so they could escape.

The gunfire ceased for the moment as the blast from the upper room became an obvious deterrent and concern for everyone. The sirens became even louder, and the law was obviously close. Miguel, grabbing his shoulder, pulled himself to his feet and yelled at his associates, "Let's get out of here!" His men began running toward the SUVs, and his lead man, assisting Miguel in a crippling fast pace, attempted to get in the door of the lead vehicle, but stumbling from weakness with the loss of blood, he tripped before finally being forced behind the driver's seat. The lead associate then jumped into the driver's seat and cranked up the engine. A police patrol unit with lights and sirens blaring pulled up in front of him. He pushed the accelerator to the floor and whipped the SUV around the patrol unit as a second unit blocked his passage. The door to the patrol unit flew open, and the officer positioned behind the car door pulled a weapon and took aim. He then, in a demanding voice, yelled, "Get out of the vehicle with your hands up," and followed with "You are surrounded." Miguel, in pain and realizing the defeat, leaned forward and told his lead man, "Give it up, and get me to a hospital."

The drone of the jetliner hummed in the background as a flight attendant addressed Rod, who was sitting in first-class seating with

Katrina next to him. She questioned, "May I get you something to drink, sir?"

Rod turned to Katrina and asked, "Would you like something?"

Katrina, with her flowing hair and a warm, adoring expression on her face, stared into Rod's eyes and in a soft tone responded, "Oh, you have no idea what I would like right now, but I will settle for a vodka and lime on ice."

Rod turned back to the attendant, who was standing patiently with a half smile, rolling her eyes, and resolved, "A vodka and lime over ice and a Jack and Coke for me." He then turned back to Katrina and in an inquiring voice questioned, "I wonder if we can get the Laredo news in Cozumel?"

Katrina, in a very sarcastic demeanor, interjected, "Rod, can we take a break from police work and Laredo for one day?"

The jail cells at the Laredo Police Department were now filled with both Victoria's and Miguel's henchmen. Victoria, in a cell all alone, screamed at the jailer, "I was attacked, and you have no reason to hold my men and me!"

The jailer responded, "It will all be worked out, Ms. Lucas, in time."

Miguel was at the local medical facility, chained to a bed and being administered to by a physician. He, in a gravelly voice, with half-slurred words, yelled out, "She killed my father, and you idiots have no idea who you are dealing with!"

Victoria, now with her face against the steel bars, in a low but demanding tone explained, "Miguel Costello, the man in your local hospital, is a cartel leader from California, and he will have all of you blown away!" She then ended with "He must be put in maximum security for everyone's safety!"

The total vacation now filled Katrina's mind as the overview of Cozumel's picturesque landscape consumed with vacationers from all around the world lined the beaches with colorful umbrellas. Rod and Katrina lay back in chaise lounge chairs at the hotel pool, each with a margarita on the side table. Rod lay back staring through his dark Ray-Ban sunglasses while Katrina, in a solid black bikini displaying her tan body, turned on her side, staring at Rod with an air of bliss. Several persons were walking past while others were sitting at tables with drinks and food. Rod, now focusing on one particular table across the pool, shifted his head with a look of wonder as he observed two individuals, a man and woman, laughing and nibbling on burgers. The more he looked, the more intent he became. He then sat up and removed his glasses from his face and with a questioning expression stated, "Can't be!"

Katrina sat up and questioned Rod's immediate concern as she asked, "Is there something wrong, Rod?"

Rod responded, with total disbelief in his voice, "My God, it's Nicholas Musso and that woman!"

ABOUT THE AUTHOR:

C.J. Savoie, a retired engineering grew up in the country amid the sugar cane fields of Louisiana and has written numerous poems and literary compositions. The Resolve marks his first fictional action story that he hopes will keep readers itching to find out what happens next.

Milton Keynes UK
Ingram Content Group UK Ltd.
UKHW010618250624
444652UK00001B/145